The Skies of Crete

The Skies of Crete

James Forman

A BELL BOOK

Farrar, Straus & Company
New York

To my father, Leo E. Forman

The Skies of Crete

꙼꙼ ꙼꙼ ꙼꙼ ꙼꙼ ꙼꙼

Early morning. Penelope slept face down with her arms out straight. The heavy square bed was made of cedar wood and fastened to the wall with wooden pegs. It was as wide as it was long and she could have slept crosswise, although she was tall. Five generations had slept in the bed, which, should it ever leave the room, would do so in broken fragments. It was too big for the door.

Penelope rolled over in her sleep. She dozed fitfully while a hungry storm traveled the night, thunder grumbling in its empty stomach. Not fully conscious, she thought the rain would be good for the crops. The year was dry. Without water the crops would wither. She might have slept again, but the noises she heard in dreams grew and trembled until they shook the house. Something enormous lunged up the farmhouse path. The hissing grass bent before it. When it leaned its gigantic weight against the walls, the timbers groaned. Glass shivered in the windowpanes. Eyes wide, Penelope lifted her head and a new noise was born in her ears, a sound which leaped from the horizon, a terrible tearing of linen into strips, magnified.

The windowpanes shuddered, and in the lightning flashes she could see cracks spreading across the glass like silver veins in a transparent leaf. Glass splintered onto the floor.

Penelope groped for a box of wooden matches, found them, snapped one match off, tried another. The flame leaped up. She touched it to the lamp wick and the flame stretched itself lazily. There was no wind to make it flicker, though the shutters were bumping. Penelope crossed the room to secure them, taking the lamp so that she would not step on the glass.

From the window she could see no flashes of lightning —not as she was accustomed to think of lightning; no yellow snakes of electricity wriggling down the clouds—but an intermittent glow radiated from the hills beyond the town. Thunder tumbled overhead, but the night was beautifully clear. Tilting her head she could see the moon was there, gilding the olive trees. Stars hung serenely above the thunder.

Gradually, voices rose through the diminishing uproar. Leaning far out through the casement, she saw shadowy figures moving up the road toward the Metaxas

4

farm; villagers seeking higher ground to discover what was happening to the world.

The storm was dying. Now there was only an occasional sound, the snap-snapping of twigs. Somewhere hundreds of twigs were being broken. Who listens at night to the crackling of twigs? Everyone in the village was listening. They crossed themselves in Aghios Miron that night, because they knew in their hearts that the sounds came from a source more deadly than any storm.

Everywhere doors and windows were opened. Lights appeared. Villagers congregated in the street and those with sturdy legs hiked past the Metaxas farm and through the olive grove to the ridge.

"What is it?" they asked one another. They gazed at the sky. There, performing their crisscross circuits, were the stars, which some believed were fire and others bits of chalk. A few believed they were gemstones in the crown of God. The stars were a wonder and something to argue over, but not this night.

Penelope strained to hear the chatter from the road.

"It's no thunderstorm," said one.

"Perhaps they're blasting somewhere," said another.

"At night? What are you thinking of? I tell you, it's an earthquake. I was almost thrown out of bed."

"What about the flashes?"

Penelope moved back into the shadows. She was in her nightclothes and did no want to be seen. The men in the street had put their trousers on hurriedly while the women had pulled skirts over their nightgowns.

"You're fooling yourselves," said a heavy male voice. "It's the enemy. They're attacking the naval base now."

"You're crazy! The way my bed trembled, it's nothing but an earthquake."

"That's right," said a woman's voice.

"At our house the pottery fell right off the shelf."

The voices in the road belonged to inky shadows, darker than the night itself. Below, in the village, lights appeared. Women thrust their heads and shoulders through the windows. Like the silhouetted puppets of the "Black Eyed" theater their voices rose, faint and full of fear. They asked for news.

"Tell me, what about the glow in the sky?"

"Fires," said someone. "Earthquakes are known to start fires."

"But not here?"

"We were lucky. It wasn't bad here."

"Isn't there anything we ought to do?"

"No, nothing. It's all over. Go back to bed."

A woman asked, "What's the time now?"

"Almost time to get up."

It was an hour before dawn on the twentieth of May.

They might have all gone home then but for the two shadows that came running. Bad news came headlong on two pairs of feet, two boys racing to tell. They drew up gasping, barely able to speak. They squatted down with their eyes shut and their breath coming and going quickly while the villagers clustered around them. Penelope could not hear what they had to say, but the responses of the villagers were clear.

"Blown to pieces? I don't believe it! The road to Heraklion bombed?"

"Nikolio's pigs killed? All the piglets bombed? You don't fight wars by bombing piglets!"

"These two are making up stories," said a woman.

"We could go," said a man. "We ought to go. Nikolio might need help."

Finally a new voice, which had in its tone something that was sorrow and something that was anger and defiance, said, "We don't need to poke about in a mess of dead pigs to know we've been bombed."

These words Penelope believed; it was her father's voice. But the others were anxious not to believe, or to see what a bomb could do to a dirt road—and what it could do to piglets. In twos and threes they scurried off, some running, until the crowd that had been mumbling and gesturing began to pound the dry ground with their bare feet. Forever afterward the sound of running feet would linger in Penelope's memory, that smacking of feet sprinting toward war.

It already smelled lightly of dawn when she turned from the window. The moon had grown pale and all was misty. A star plummeted across the brightening haze and dropped into the eastern glow. Dawn and the lamp balanced one another, seeming to make less light together than either might make alone. Penelope lifted the lamp to her lips and gently blew it out.

part one

one

❦❦❦❦❦❦

Early in April 1941, there
was no thunder to awaken
the sleepers. Then it was quiet. There is no quieter time
than when the dew is forming. Penelope smiled in her
sleep and, sensing the smile and wondering why it was
there, opened her eyes. A whisper stirred the hush and the
girl rose. She padded soundlessly across the packed earth
floor of the dusky farmhouse to pause, listening, before
the huge carved door. She pressed the latch with both
hands. As though a strong ghost shoved it, the door swung

inward, blown by a warm breeze. Penelope's pulse beat faster as she stepped into the predawn silence. A total grayness emptied the world: no mountains, no village, no far-off coast, only a star blinking like a drop of wine over the Aegean Sea.

The wind breathed from the east, tousling her dark hair, blowing her skirt back like a banner. The Cucumber Wind, ripener of crops, had arrived in the night. Spring had come.

A drab white radiance spread east and west. Behind the mountains of Lasithi, the sun was climbing hand over fist. Through an eternity of white-black days, Crete had waited while the gales raced down the sky. Penelope had waited for the Cucumber Wind and now it brushed her, explored her clothes, tunneled down to her eardrums, tingled her scalp. When she breathed, she tasted the wind, blending plowed fields, lemon blossoms and melted snow.

She gave a loud tremulous call, to no person but to the air. Dizzy with spring, she began the first jarring steps of a dance, whirling, almost defying the law of gravity. Again she gave the cry. This time she awakened the Metaxas' rooster. The bird opened his round red eyes and glared furiously at what was happening in the sky, beat with his rusty wings, puffed out his chest and crowed. Angrily, repeatedly, he called for the sun. Job, the donkey, sniffed the dew-fresh earth, raised his tail bolt upright and brayed. Before the morning star had faded, Penelope's message was answered and reanswered throughout the hillside town of Aghios Miron and beyond. Animal voices clamored across the length and breadth of Crete, announcing, "Spring is come. The Cucumber Wind is here."

For a moment, Penelope was conscious only of her body, the bumping heart, the racing blood, and the wind wrapping her round. Then there came the crunch of booted feet, and a towering individual with blue-black beard stalked from the shadows. The dancing girl did not see him until she was caught and held.

"Slow down, Pen," he said. "You'll need that strength today. We've got a long way to go."

Normally he called her Penny. His pet term was Pen, and in rare moments of exasperation, Penelope. But Emmanuel was seldom annoyed, particularly with his only daughter, his only child. They did not look alike, these two, the father with his villainous black eyebrows and bushy head, the girl almost delicate. She had her mother's steady olive eyes, so large they dominated her face, the dainty nostrils and the firm lower lip that had stamped the family as quality folk when they first came to Crete in a caïque. But father and daughter had a rare understanding. They scarcely needed to speak.

"It's really here at last," he said. "Just smell it!" He took a deep breath.

Emmanuel looped his arm about his daughter's shoulders. Four hundred phantom generations of Cretan farmers stood then in their shoes, remembering similar mornings. They shared the springtime, the weathered farmer looking back on many such occasions, the girl savoring the Cucumber Wind as though it had never come before.

Finally he said, "Spring, you know, comes by way of the sea. One morning the sky seems bluer, the wind is a little warmer and spring steps ashore clad in flowers, cherry blossoms in her hair and the new lambs following behind her. . . ."

How many times had Penelope heard her father say the same thing? She looked into his dark fierce face, a little craftily from under her eyebrows, to make him smile.

Wrinkles of good nature radiating from the corners of his eyes betrayed him. His dark eyes were never fierce and his slow voice was good to hear.

"And in her hands she carries a swallow's nest, gently, so the eggs won't crack. That's how spring comes to the olive groves. Spring even visits the cemeteries, planting poppies among the stones. Yes, it's a grand morning when spring arrives. Those that come after are only second best."

He stooped, took up a handful of soil and smelled it. Every spring Emmanuel fell in love with the land. "Even the ground knows," he said. "Yesterday it had a dead and dusty smell."

"It's a growing smell," Penelope said. "Yes, a great green growing smell."

A shrill shout broke the spell. It came from the house with all the urgency of a fire siren. Her mother's voice. Penelope had no pet name for Katerina; not that she did not love the imperious voice shouting from the doorway. It was the love a soldier might have for a most trusted though somewhat distant officer. As long as Penelope could remember, Emmanuel had obeyed his wife's mandates with willing good humor and when Old Markos, Penelope's grandfather, was not away prowling the hills, he obeyed too, growlingly, as a tiger obeys its trainer.

The voice came again, sounding as if Katerina had been running up many flights to announce that the house was ablaze. Of course this was unlikely, since the Metaxas house was made of stone and clay and had no stairs except a ladder to the loft.

Obediently Emmanuel trudged off. Reluctant to surrender the first morning of spring, Penelope followed around the corner of the house. There was Katerina waiting in the doorway, sturdy as an anvil, shaking her head because they did not run. She was small with tight dark skin and handsome strong arms, though if Penelope had been asked to describe her mother she might have said she was a large person. When she thought of her parents together, she realized they were an odd pair, her father big and almost lumbering, Katerina moving on her toes with the grace of a Japanese wrestler. The farm they had fashioned from this eroded hillside was the most fertile in Aghios Miron. Penelope shared their pride. She could be happy nowhere else and had no desire to travel. Katerina had often explained the feeling: what was the good in seeing beloved things shamed by grander sights? The war was still far away, but there was talk of invading armies and bombers. Katerina had vowed she would rather die than leave her home. Penelope felt the same, though her father would only say, "We have to wait and see."

Once inside, Penelope waited while Katerina scrutinized her husband, flicked a fleck of dust from his multipleated trousers. Penelope thought he looked like an overgrown boy having his ears forcibly scoured. Katerina stepped back.

"You'll do; yes, you'll do splendidly," she said, smiling suddenly. The charming smile did not fit her brusque manner. It took Penelope by surprise. There were so many things about her mother that were unexpected.

Thus dismissed, Emmanuel withdrew. Bruising the floor with his boots, he squeezed rather than walked through the doorway. Katerina muttered to herself, but she was still smiling.

"I can't hear what you're saying," Penelope told her.

"I was just thinking this house seemed a lot bigger when we built it." And then reflectively, "It doesn't seem large enough for him—or me, for that matter. And you're getting to be such a big thing. We could add a room or two at the back. Now there'll be the boy."

"Alexis!" Penelope tried out the name with the same pleasure she might experience on opening a Christmas gift. "Do you think he'll be good-looking?"

Until the letter arrived saying that Alexis was sailing to Crete because of the war, Penelope had never given a thought to her cousin. He had been no more than a tinted and fading baby picture, gathering dust on a shelf. Now the picture lay on the family table with a letter. It gave no hint of the changes so many years might bring, nor did the letter, a hasty scrawl on lined notepaper asking for sanctuary. It bore no return address and no other information. The boy was simply on his way. Under the circumstances no choice remained for a family whose greatest pride was hospitality. Penelope and her father were going to meet the boat.

"You'd think he would have stayed and fought," said Penelope.

"He's just your age. He's fifteen."

"So? I would have," and when Katerina contradicted her she said, "I would have, if I were a boy. And his father's an evzone, so he must be brave and good-looking. Is his father handsome?"

"You know very well all the Metaxas men are handsome . . . and too courageous for their own good, I'm afraid."

Penelope discounted the sadness in her mother's voice. No one could be too brave, and in her mind's eye she saw the dawn-gray mountains of Albania and the evzones swooping down with their fierce war cry, "Aera! Aera!" Alexis was in the front rank. Then she said, "Mother, will you answer me one thing, honestly?"

"I never answer you in any other way."

"Mother, do you think I'm pretty?"

"Naturally you are. You've the best features of both of us. Now I've got work to do."

"But Mother, that's not what I mean. What I want to know is, am I *pretty?*"

"That's what I just told you. You have a very nice young face, just the way it ought to look. Now get along with your father."

"Oh, Mother, you don't tell the truth about anything!"

"That's right; I'm a frightful liar and you're the ugliest girl in the world," said Katerina, who had watched Penelope grow from a chubby toddler dragging at Emmanuel's arm to a girl so lovely she might be taken for one of the Nereides, the spell-casters, the spinners of moonlight.

Penelope asked, "What was it like when you and Papa first met? I mean, what did he do?"

"He got on with his work," Katerina said, "without chattering so much."

She picked up a short-handled broom and began whisking impatiently. Penelope watched her until Katerina held out the broom, handle first. "Would you rather have my job?" was all she said. Penelope backed toward the door, opened it, shut it and was gone.

Emmanuel waited there, and with him, Job. The burro was small and soft to touch. His hide was cottony but his frame was solid as steel and his eyes had the sparkle of jet mirrors. They called him Job for his misfortunes: nests of yellow jackets hidden beneath his hoofs, lead lines twined about his legs. The blue beads he wore about his neck did no good. The evil eye was constantly upon him.

They started down toward the old Heraklion road. The burro pulled a creaking cart painted carnival colors and Emmanuel walked with his arm resting on the burro's rump. The town still reverberated with the din of roosters and in the doorways old men stood rubbing their hands together, feeling the warm wind in their bones. Beyond the town they took the city road. Such ships were never early; they ambled along down the middle of the road without any fear of cars or buses bursting through the haze which slowly withdrew from the silvery olive trees. On the hills flocks of sheep clustered like gold scarabs, their bells muted by the mist.

"I haven't been to Heraklion in almost a year," said Penelope.

"Not since the raisin crop last September. It's easy to hibernate in Aghios Miron. Too easy."

"Why do you say 'too easy'?"

"We're not bears that can afford to sleep the winter away in a cave, or cranes that disappear into Africa, nobody knows where. We can't hide ourselves away in these hills, not in times like these."

"I don't see why not. There's no place I want to go."

It had never occurred to Penelope that there might be more to see in the world than her island. Crete had everything: sea, mountains, fertile plains. As for cities, there was Heraklion, basking like some old serpent in the brazen light of morning. Far off, the first rays touched the cupolas of the churches, and soon they would reach the houses, the small yards and damp alleys.

"You probably don't remember my brother very well," said Emmanuel.

"Alexis' father, with the beard like Saint Nicholas? I remember the beard and the radio he brought. I wish you had kept the radio."

"It was things like the radio that took him away from

us," said Emmanuel, his voice rising with anger. "Imagine a Greek listening to a radio and deciding he was needed to fight a war in Spain. That's why I didn't keep it. I didn't want it doing such things to me, but I know now you can't hide forever."

"I certainly remember the radio," said Penelope, smiling to herself. Emmanuel's voice had faded in her ears, a gurgling stream half-heard as she recalled the shiny new box with its knobs and the glass bottles glowing in the back. It had been the first radio in the village. There were others now, but the old one still played. Emmanuel had given it to the village and it was always blaring there, under the tree called Idleness, where old men sat and sipped Turkish coffee from little white cups.

"What can a man, one man, do about the world, anyway?" said Emmanuel. "If it weren't for radios and airplanes we could get along up here. Now it doesn't seem as though we can keep strangers out of our affairs any more."

"You're thinking about the war and why Alexis is coming."

Emmanuel said, "Yes, there's the war, but the war's only part of something bigger."

"If the enemy comes, will we fight them?" asked Penelope.

"Pen, how should I know? There's still the sea between us. We just have to wait."

"Markos will fight. I bet Alexis will too. And I'm a pretty good shot; you said so."

"Sometimes you don't sound as old as you look, Penny," he said. "When women start fighting, that's time for the men to give up. And just because your grandfather talks about the old days full of banners and glory, that isn't the way it is now. That hasn't got anything to do with bombers."

"I wasn't talking about bombers," said Penelope.

"Let's not talk about it at all," said her father. "It will be real enough with your cousin here. He'll talk about nothing else."

War was not an easy thing for Penelope to visualize. It seemed the private possession of her grandfather, who brought it out on wintry nights with its curved swords and flapping flags, like pictures carefully etched in a history book. He told of the great days when Crete had broken away from Turkey, of his own heedless courage, a quality she took for granted in every man. That was war—to stalk through glancing shot and shell with a tidy bandage around your head which covered a wound no more lethal than a hornet's sting. Such war was majestic, but what had it to do with this business of bombers? She had heard about the bombing of Suda Bay and she realized what explosives could do. She knew that fishermen used dynamite sticks illegally to catch sardines and she had seen what happened to hands which had not thrown the sticks fast enough, but she could not imagine dynamite falling out of the sky except in a very gray and hazy way. Whatever was real for Penelope would appear behind her eyes in vivid colors. The hands of the fishermen were red, as were her grandfather's stories, red and gold, but the bombers were gray in a gray sky, dropping sticks of dynamite on gray towns where gray people ran about waving their gray arms.

From the foot of the hills the road led straight and flat toward the city walls and the Kanea gate. Others were plodding along the road on foot while a row of worn-out buses stood beside the gate. Only the coast road was good enough for the buses, but no peasants with bumping bundles issued from them now. There was no gasoline to spare. Someday, when the war was over, Penelope resolved to ride in a bus.

They passed between weed-grown bastions of the old fortress, where engraved Venetian lions reared in moldering defiance. A damp tunnel swallowed them and giggled back at their clicking feet. Once Penelope would have shrieked to hear the tunnel answer. Now she had dignity. She was about to meet her cousin. She held her tongue.

Within the walls, Broad Street was lined with clapboard wooden shops. Cobblers, coopers, apprentices filled the air with hammering, explosive laughter and the gasping breath of bellows. Heraklion was a spectacular sight for a girl from a hill town. What joys could the rest of the world hold? Surely, for Penelope, this world was large enough.

With Emmanuel she let herself be jostled toward the main square. There were the glass and china shops and the trees. They drifted across the square toward 1821 Street, pausing beside a phonograph which sat on a chair in the middle of the street and played a cracked record. Penelope would have given anything for such a machine. Then a loudspeaker began broadcasting the war news, first in Greek, then in other languages. They turned the corner to the food markets which spilled out into the road. Bits of ragged awning deflected the sun, but nothing, not even the long strips of sticky paper, defeated the flies. Butchers lounged behind wooden chopping blocks, their crimson aprons touching the ground. Behind them, whole pigs, whole sheep dangled, hooked and split open the length of their pale bodies to display the solid fat and pink meat.

She sidestepped a street barber shop where mingled beards and locks flowed down the gutter in a trickle of slow suds toward the harbor. The ship might arrive at any time now, and they walked quickly along the quay where corks and scraps of wood bobbed on the water in a thick yellow scum. Emmanuel asked a porter about the refugee ship. The porter asked a fisherman. No one knew. Perhaps it had stopped at Skyros for repairs. One fisherman joined his hands, tore them apart explosively. Perhaps a submarine, who could say? Penelope scanned the horizon. Strangely, in the heat she felt a sudden chill, picturing the ship drawing steadily closer, like fate, bringing with it all the miseries of a world she did not wish to acknowledge. Yet it was still a sunny day and the little waves lapped laughingly along the mole.

They sat down to wait, and became the only stationary objects on the bustling quay where dealers, sailors and boatmen swarmed among the cans of oil and casks of wine and piles of rubbish, shouting, cursing, loading and unloading in a hurry.

The Old Harbor was guarded by the Venetian fortress, gray, rumpled and stitched together with pitted stone and crumbling plaster. It resembled a vast sleeping hippopotamus. Emmanuel hunched himself against the seawall. A string of amber worry beads moved one by one through his fingers.

"Job's limping," he said. "Did you notice?"

Penelope nodded vaguely. Job always had something wrong and she was thinking about her cousin, picturing him in brilliant colors, tall as a sapling. The son of an evzone would have to be tall, and tanned by the weather. Evzones never slept under a roof. They did not shiver in the cold, not even in the mountains of Albania.

"I'd take him by the blacksmith's now," said Emmanuel, "but we can't be sure when the boat will get in." The beads clicked over his palm, but Penelope didn't hear him. She dwelt in an imaginary future. There would be so much to show Alexis. There would be so many things for them to do. Then she wilted. How could the young and dashing warrior of her imaginings have the slightest interest in her? Only last winter had she given up braids. The happy future was ruined, and her attention shifted back to the quay and a loud ringing voice which came from a thrown-back head with a wide-open throat. A koulouria vendor was proclaiming his sesame-seed rolls, balanced in precarious columns atop a wooden board. Many were the drachmas squandered in the hope that a bun chosen from the bottom of the stack would cause the lot to tumble. She laughed silently, thinking of how it would be and then remembered Alexis, who would not laugh at such foolishness. She told herself to think of something serious. She thought of war, of wounded heroes with drops of blood as big as strawberries on their starched and ruffled shirtfronts. She remembered the refugee ship and looked toward the western horizon. Rowboats, fishing boats, sailing caïques. Far off she saw a wisp of smoke and faintly a whistle sounded. A sailor from the headland shouted, "A ship, ahoy!"

two

꿔꿔꿔꿔꿔

The refugee ship cleared the end of the mole, listing far over with the weight of passengers along the starboard rail. The crowd on the dock grew, pressed together against the debarkation fence. They stood on tiptoe, expectant. The ship grew closer.

Penelope could distinguish faces jammed together above the rail. People near her began waving in the Greek manner, palm outward as though shaking their fists in anger. Some passengers waved back, but not many. They had brought the sorrow of Greece to the island.

After backing and coming forward again, the ship butted against the mole. Lines were secured fore and aft. The gangplank rolled out. The refugees piled ashore with babies and shapeless bundles and trunks. They were all very old or very young except for the soldiers, many of whom were carried or moved laboriously on crutches. Many hands and feet were bandaged, and she recalled stories of soldiers injuring themselves to escape from war. Could they all be cowards? Only later was she to learn the truth. These were men who had fought in the mountains where winter never dies. Frostbite, not bullets, had felled them. Penelope, who had known no real suffering, watched them, and the waiting crowd, as though she were not one of them. Those who had had no previous contact with war were shocked into silence by a closer view of the passengers. Fear and weariness were in those faces, and a hopelessness mute beyond communication. For a moment, war set miles between those who waited and those who poured from the ship. Then they were blood kin again, rushing together, finding those to whom they belonged. Groups formed. Penelope began to see some who were not going to find their people. They went from group to group, repeating names, looking, asking questions. They milled about, or sat dumbly on suitcases or coils of rope. Somewhere a baby began to cry.

Penelope closed her eyes to steady herself. "I'm sick," she thought, but with no usual sickness. When she opened her eyes again the crowd was still there, and through it pressed Emmanuel. With him came a boy.

Alexis, drawn over at a tipsy angle by the weight of a huge suitcase, was not as she had imagined. The total effect of him was white and yellow: flesh pale as talcum, hair tawny as sun-bleached autumn grass. He was frail; he must not have spent a great many hours out of doors.

They faced each other.

Emmanuel said quietly, "Penelope, this is Alexis."

"Hello, Penelope," said the boy. There was a strangeness in his accent which emphasized all the *e* sounds in her name. It sounded very romantic and the girl was momentarily charmed. She held out her hand. Alexis tried to shift the suitcase to his left hand but there was no room. He set the bag down, clenching and unclenching the hand that had held it. "It's fearfully heavy," he said apologetically, and Penelope looked at the newcomer as she would at a square egg.

"Well, then," said Emmanuel heartily, "is that the lot?"

"No, sir," said Alexis. "I've another parcel over there," and when Emmanuel offered to carry it, Alexis protested. He went alone. Penelope watched him rooting through the confusion of odds and ends where the sailors had lowered luggage in a net. Even at a distance, his blond hair was as unmistakable as a bonfire.

"He seems like a nice polite young man," said Emmanuel.

"But he's so young and sick-looking; he's such a queer color, white like that."

Emmanuel said, "He's partly Scottish, you know."

"Are they all pale and sickly?"

"Yes, of course," said Emmanuel. "It's a hard land without much sun, just cold mist and early evenings. Now that's enough. He's coming back."

Alexis returned with a parcel wrapped in butcher's paper. "This your mule?" he asked and Emmanuel nodded.

"Nice fellow," said Alexis, stroking Job's neck. "Looks like he's hurt his leg, the way he's holding it."

"He's thrown a shoe," said Penelope. "We'll go by the blacksmith's. He'll be all right."

"Think you can walk for a while?" asked Emmanuel. "I'll take that luggage off your hands." Again Alexis insisted on carrying his own things. He had managed through Greece, in carts, on the back of a tank, on foot. He would manage now, though he tottered under his burden, seeming to lift the entire earth with each step. Penelope offered to take one end with him but Alexis brushed her aside.

"You're a strange one," she told him, and walked on ahead.

Torgut's shop was on the street of metal workers. An old Turk, he had fought for the Pasha during the revolution in which Crete had broken away from Turkish rule. How he had exchanged shots with her grandfather was a story Penelope knew by heart. She could have told how they became friends later on, and more. They had slashed each other's wrists and mingled their blood. Now the blood brothers were old men and their glory was legend. Yet she knew Torgut was still the best smith on the island. Big as a bull, red as a watermelon, his arm had become pillar-thick from constant pounding. Bellowing, he emerged to greet his friends, and the shop was lost behind him.

"Emmanuel!" he cried. "This is good!" They clasped hands ferociously. He welcomed Penelope with a suffocating hug, then pretended she had cracked his ribs. "I'm only joking, Penny," he said. "If I were fifty years younger, I'd come courting."

A spot of red appeared in both her cheeks. She shook her head as if to deny the compliment, saying, "You must meet my cousin Alexis."

They greeted with a dignified pumping of hands and the smith asked about the war, something Penelope had hesitated to do. Alexis spoke reluctantly. He had gone out of Grevena at night with an oxcart but the oxen had gone lame. Everyone had been fleeing. The roads were full of soldiers, Greek and English. An English tank had permitted him to ride but the tank had broken a tread. They had abandoned the tank and again it was walking and running to find shelter where there was no shelter when the planes came down. After passing Thermopylae it had been better. After that there were only the planes to worry about. There had been no fear of being surrounded.

To all of this Torgut listened gravely, his one good ear turned toward Alexis. The other, as though from some ghastly shaving mishap, had altogether vanished. "Pray Allah they hold them back at Thermopylae," he said.

Alexis said, "My father may be there."

"It's just like the Three Hundred Spartans turning back the Persians," said Penelope, thrilled to think of history repeating itself.

Alexis gave her a gloomy look.

Too late, Penelope remembered the fatal epitaph left to mark that ancient fight: *Stranger, bear this message to the Spartans, that we lie here obedient to their laws.* The three hundred had given their lives to a man. "I'm sorry," she whispered, but Alexis spoke not a word.

In the end, Torgut did the talking. He pictured Greece as little David confronting Goliath, a Nazi giant. David might be brave, he said, but David was out of stones. Torgut spat on the ground as straight and hard as a beanshooter and then glared at the spot. "Things were different when I was a boy. Your grandfather, he'll tell you that. David used to have a chance."

28

The street was filling with shadows before Job was finally shod and the cart loaded. Torgut sat back watching them sleepily, the flexible stem of a glass-bowled water pipe passing snakily between his pink lips. "These Greeks, all impatience," he muttered.

Emmanuel said, "We'd like to stay and chat, but it's late, and the boy . . . he's had a hard time."

"I know, I know, my friend," said Torgut, standing up. In a confidential voice, one which touched on the heart of their relationship, he said, "Mark my words, it's worse than the radio's letting on. I know on good authority. We're in for it, sooner or later." With his finger he stabbed the front of Emmanuel's shirt. "Be prepared."

This had not been meant for Penelope's ears, but she had heard. It made her want to do something important. She didn't know what.

Finally they left the Turk to his pipe and turned again into Broad Street. The avenue was filled afresh with donkey carts, heaped high with wood, charcoal, bottles of olive oil and wine, baskets of bread and brass jars of honey flashing like tiny suns. So many were the donkeys that Penelope knew them as the Cretan railroad, the only one on the island.

The traffic passed through the stone arch and Penelope, observing the serious boy with his tight pale lips trudging beside her, could not imagine him ever shouting to make the walls ring with echoes. In the dusky light the Venetian lions glowed red above the battlements. Here the roads fanned out and the Metaxas went south toward snowy Ida, glowing in the distance.

Alexis asked Penelope if it was very far, and she told him to ride if he felt tired. "Emmanuel won't mind if you want to. Don't be ashamed."

"I was just curious," said Alexis.

"We'll be home by dark or a little after," she told him.

"A couple of miles, then, I guess," said the boy.

"I guess," said Penelope. For her a mile had nothing to do with feet or yards. It was the distance traveled by a donkey in an hour.

They climbed steadily, Emmanuel in the lead, flicking a twig at Job to keep him moving. Penelope kept her eyes on her plodding cousin. He was a disappointment, though she knew he must be tired and homesick. With rest he might improve, but never to the level of her former imaginings. It was impossible for Penelope to understand what it would be like to be a stranger in a strange country.

The brassy rays of the sun still slanted over their faces, caught their foreheads, noses and hands so that they looked more like bronze statues than people.

"It looks like an orange," said Penelope, breaking the long silence.

"What does?" said Alexis, walking closer to her.

"The sun. Or maybe more like a red August tomato."

"It looks to me like a bomb exploding," said Alexis.

"Then bombs must be quite beautiful."

"No, ugly. There is nothing uglier."

But Penelope could not help thinking it must be a little bit beautiful if it looked so much like the sun.

"I'd say you lived a long way back," said Alexis.

"Quite far," said Penelope, "but not as far as you can go. Grandfather has wandered around the mountains for years, and he says he hasn't seen it all. You'd be amazed how gigantic Crete is. Some parts of it are still as wild as a jungle. Once it was all that way, even the people, but Crete isn't like that now, not mostly. Mostly I guess it's just like everywhere else."

"That's too bad."

"What's bad about it?" asked Penelope.

"Well, nothing, but I thought, the way you sounded, you were sad about it getting like other places. That's why I said it's too bad."

Penelope kept going with the same long springing strides, but now Alexis kept up beside her.

"Do you know any people that still are wild?"

"Not really," answered Penelope, "but some people say they've seen centaurs, up near Mount Ida. They're really only goats."

"Then it's just myths, make-believe?"

"I didn't say that. They're the shepherds; some of them are as wild as goats. I saw a shepherd boy once with pointed ears bounding away like a rabbit. That's the truth, and wait till you meet El Greco. No one knows where he comes from."

"I can hardly wait," said Alexis, skeptically. He winced as he walked. There was very little left of his shoes, but when Emmanuel offered him a ride, he again declined.

Alexis said, "Well, anyway, it's hot enough. You'd think it would cool off this time of day."

"Oh, it will," she assured him. "By the time we're home you'll be shivering."

"It's lots colder where I come from," said Alexis. "I'm used to shivering."

"The weather must have been terrible to frostbite so many poor soldiers," said Penelope.

"It was wonderful weather," said Alexis. "There were blizzards for almost a week."

"Then how can you say it was wonderful?" said Penelope, annoyed now. From the first he did not have the heroic shape of her imaginings. Now he revealed a callous soul as well.

"Because it kept the planes down. Otherwise, I probably wouldn't be here at all, and neither would they. It was really wonderful weather."

Penelope did not know Alexis well enough to believe him. Surely no world could be so savage that half-frozen men look to the skies and pray for snow.

"Anyway, I wish my feet were like yours, used to going barefoot," said Alexis. It was a relief to laugh at Alexis' feet, those shoes from which the toes protruded like turtles emerging from their shells. "I hate to see them falling apart. You'd never guess where they came from."

"Athens?"

"No, from London."

"London, England?"

"I was there once with my mother. She's a nurse, you know. Well, that was a long time ago; you can tell by the shoes."

"What's London like?" Penelope asked.

"It's very full," he said, "just like Crete's empty."

They walked the rest of the way without the sun. The ditches beside the road seemed to grow deeper as they filled with darkness. Emmanuel flicked Job with his stick and drove the burro hard, directing him around corners with loud shouts. He flailed the stick in the air with frightening vigor, but except for that first gentle tap never touched the drooping burro, whose pace was scarcely accelerated by the commotion.

It was night when they reached the farmhouse. Emmanuel unhitched the burro and stroked Job's long nose and fed him a few dried figs from the palm of his hand.

"You're a frail little fellow, Job," he said, "to pull such heavy loads."

Katerina met them at the door. "My poor boy!" she cried, then clasped Alexis and kissed him. "I was afraid you might not get here."

"There wasn't anywhere else for me to go," said Alexis; then, because this sounded ungracious, "I mean, it was fine of you to take me in."

Within, the house smelled of quince and cypress. At the far end was a wide, crackling fireplace with cooking implements hung around it. On the mantle were a clock, a china dog, a gaudy painting of the Crucifixion and a tinted photograph of a young bearded man wearing bandoliers across his chest and a gigantic horse pistol in his belt. "That's your grandfather," said Penelope with pride in her voice. "He'll be back any day."

Alexis looked at the picture. He did not seem charmed by his grandfather's level stare.

The rest of the room was simple: earthenware jars lined the walls and from the rafters hung strings of quince, sage, red peppers and rosemary. In the center, a table with four wooden chairs was set for supper. Dark doorways led to other rooms, four in all, while a ladder pierced the ceiling to the loft. It was the largest house in Aghios Miron.

"You'll have the loft," Penelope told him. "It's a grand place, just like a castle being up there above everything."

"You must be starving," interrupted Katerina.

"What I really am is thirsty," said Alexis, and he told them it had been weeks since he had tasted clean water. Listening, Penelope could not imagine how bombing might pollute water so that its taste was sickening. In Aghios Miron, water came from mountain springs, deep and green and cool. She poured Alexis a glass full from the clay amphora and he drank it down with the Lenten meal of grilled fish and greens. Meat was forbidden. Alexis blew on his food and stared at it like a miser contemplating a heap of gold. Then he began to eat.

"There's plenty more, Alexis" said Penelope. "You don't have to wolf it down."

"It feels good in my stomach."

"But you'll make yourself sick."

Alexis said, "I'm eating fast, but I won't forget any of it."

When the last bit of bread had sopped up the last drop of oil, Penelope and her mother cleared the table. Afterward they chattered together, the family and their guest, about inconsequential things. It scarcely seemed possible to Penelope that war mushroomed all about their sheltered island, or that one of them had actually emerged from under its dark cloud. If only Alexis' eyes would cease to rove about the room as though he had just awakened in a strange place. She tried to arrest his eyes with her own steady gaze.

Then something happened, as unexpected and shocking as the discharge of a cannon.

Alexis seemed to turn to stone. The last trace of blood drained from his cheeks and he stared in horror at the night-blackened window. His hands flew to his face and with a gurgling sound issuing from his throat he collapsed from sight under the table.

"My Lord!" said Emmanuel. "He must have overeaten. Give me a hand."

"That's not it. Look, there," said Penelope. "See, at the window."

Behind the frame moved a huge white head, distorted by the shadows and the glass. Emmanuel laughed loudly and lay back in his chair while Penelope poked her head under the table. There was a funny smile on her face, the corners of her mouth pulled down tight. She felt like laughing, but checked herself. Alexis was crouching, hands over head, in utter panic.

"It's only Job," she whispered. "Don't be such a fool, Alexis."

Mournful old Job pressed against the pane, gazing, quiet and wistful, at the warm bright room and the members of his family.

"Come on out, Alexis," said Penelope, her hand on his shoulder.

"Just leave me alone," hissed the boy. He remained on the floor, beneath the table at which his adopted family waited, confused and horrified. Why had this happened? What sort of boy had come to live with them?

Penelope said, "We were talking about centaurs on the way. Maybe he's superstitious."

"He's not that way," said Katerina. "I can tell. He's a level-thinking boy who doesn't bother himself about that kind of foolishness."

"Well, he's had some kind of shock," said Emmanuel. "Shouldn't we do something?"

"Just let him be."

So the elders sat quietly wondering and Penelope wanted to put Alexis out of her mind. She could not. She was embarrassed for him, embarrassed by her own inability to help. She got up and walked across the room to the window. Job had gone. There was nothing but the reflection of her face and the room behind. Presently in the glass she saw Alexis reappear, white and crestfallen.

"You're all right now?" asked Emmanuel.

Alexis said he was fine. He had made a mistake, that

was all, but when he brushed the hair from his forehead Penelope saw that the fingers trembled, and when he took a glass of water, the liquid made little ripples on the surface because he could not keep it still.

"We haven't any centaurs here, not really," Penelope assured him.

"No, no, it wasn't that. I don't believe in myths. Honestly, I'm fine now. Let's not talk about it."

They did not speak of it again, though it was so obviously in all their minds that no conversation could get started. Emmanuel made a little popping noise with his lips as he drew on a cigarette. That was the only sound. "Well," he said in a hearty tone, "I'm off to bed, myself." With both hands slapping his knees, he got up.

"We're all of us exhausted," said Katerina. "Penny, you'll show Alexis his room. Go along, Alexis. You must be ready to drop."

With a lamp in one hand Penelope climbed to the loft, sure as a monkey. Alexis followed. The place smelled sweetly of wood and fresh grass. Penelope held the lamp at arm's length. There was a cot in the corner and Alexis sat down on it. Rope springs resisted his weight. He began wearily undoing his luggage.

"I'll leave the lamp," she told him. "You think you'll be all right if I go down?"

"If you'd get that funny look off your face I'd be fine," he replied.

"It's only that you seem so pale, and after what happened and all. . . ."

"Forget it," said Alexis.

"You wouldn't like another blanket or something?"

"No."

"But you're so pale; you might get a chill."

36

"Look," he said, "I'm always pale. I've had to develop a thick skin and the blood doesn't show through."

Penelope said, "I've never seen anyone who's been bombed before. You must be terribly homesick."

"I miss my parents."

"You must miss Grevena—your home."

"I hate it. I'm never going back there, never."

"But Alexis. . . ."

"Let me be. All these questions!" He turned back to his unpacking. Penelope started down.

"Good night," she whispered. "Good night, Alexis."

"Don't go," he said. "I'm sorry. I must sound awfully unfriendly, and you people are being so generous with me."

"That's all right. We know what you've been through. We wouldn't expect you to act like everybody else."

"But I *am* like everybody else," he protested. "At least I used to be." His voice had a rough edge. "You said a minute ago you'd never seen anyone who'd been in the war. What difference do you see in my face?"

"Oh, I don't know . . . you've a kind face, Alexis. I like it."

"You're lying to be nice. What do you see?"

"You didn't want to talk about it before," said Penelope.

"Go ahead and say what you're thinking!"

Penelope was perplexed. She put one foot on top of the other and stared down at them. Then she lifted her face and said abruptly, "You're not a coward, Alexis, I know that, but I think you must have had a terrible fright. You look afraid."

"Because of what happened downstairs?"

"That, and just the look you have. I don't know. Why

37

ask me? I don't know anything. If you want to talk about it, I'll listen."

Alexis stood before the tiny window. He stared and stared at the blackness outside.

"There'll be a moon," said Penelope.

There was moisture on the pane and Alexis drew a double cross with his finger and rubbed it out again. He slumped with his palm resting on the glass. Then he said, "It's like I'd always been walking along these dusty roads and hiding in caves, or looking out of black windows waiting for something. I'm sounding melodramatic, aren't I?" He forced a laugh.

"You'll see a full moon tonight."

"Do you know what I thought, downstairs, when I saw the burro outside?"

Penelope was silent.

"Have you ever seen a man with a gas mask pulled over his head? Those awful pale frog eyes and that rubber trunk dangling down? It's horrible," said Alexis, swinging suddenly to face her. "It's horrible to remember a thing like that," and this for Alexis was only the beginning of a more ghastly memory he could scarcely disclose even to himself. Then he laughed, without mirth. "Now you're the one that looks afraid!"

Penelope was afraid. Until she fell asleep that night with the moonlight turning her face a ghostly gray, there was a hollow fear inside her. She prayed for her grandfather to come home and set things right, to help her understand war and courage and not being afraid. Trying to sleep, she seemed to hear the skittering of gigantic rats, slimy and wet and chill, gnawing at the house around her, scurrying up timbers of darkness. "There are no rats," she told herself. "Think of nice thoughts, pretend that elves and fairies are playing there, and there the angels sit, guarding each corner of my bed——" But it was no good pretending and she did not open her eyes or look out the casement window, although the grove behind the house was visible. Above it a black cloud like a gigantic hen laid the moon, an egg of gold, upon the hill.

three

✴✴ ✴✴ ✴✴ ✴✴ ✴✴

O n Sunday a bell rang in
Aghios Miron. Somewhere
in the damp recesses of the little chapel a priest swung on
the bell rope. The sound bounced off the stone walls, off
the whitewashed houses. The villagers came out and
trudged down the rocky lanes to listen to the priest.

Inside, the dusky chapel was warm with the closeness
of people and the smell of candle wax. When Penelope and
Alexis arrived they stood with the rest of the congregation,
shifting from one foot to the other in the stained-glass light

that transformed them into multicolored harlequins, dappled red and blue and yellow. The singing and the chants went on while incense smoke rose to the ceiling in billows, making them cough.

When the priest appeared he was clad in blue-and-white robes, the colors of Greece. Penelope tried to concentrate on his words but could not, for he talked in the sacred language, so difficult to understand. Her eyes wandered upward with the smoke, over the length of towering silver candlesticks, up the walls covered with smoke-dulled pictures of saints and angels. In the vault, so dark and grimed that she could sense rather than see Him there, God overlooked them all from a mighty throne. Penelope shivered as she felt the power of it all. This chapel was truly blessed. Here the halt and the blind might come to discard their crutches, to shed their darkness. None could doubt it, for the walls were lined with abandoned crutches, the rafters were hung with hammered silver eyes, all gifts from the cured. It was her good fortune to have such a chapel and when the congregation faced the east to pray, Penelope gave thanks for her good life and for the good times to come. She prayed too for Alexis, that the hurt within him would heal in this good place.

Once outside it seemed to her the healing process had already begun. He seemed lighter on his feet, his lips were held less tightly. "I've only seen this town of yours in the dark," he said, "and I'd like to see your farm, too."

"Then come on. There's a place up above the olive groves where there's a marvelous view of everything."

"Everything?"

"The whole world! Come on."

"I'll race you!"

Alexis was off in the lead, but Penelope gained despite

his efforts. The shreds of his shoes had dried as stiff as wood and hurt him. He had to stop.

"Say, you can run!" he said.

"Yes, I'm a fast one. Not much to carry," she said, "and long legs to carry it. They used to call me Atalanta."

"The princess who lost the race?"

To which Penelope added, "To win herself three golden apples and a prince. Not bad for second best."

Then she pointed out every single thing on the Metaxas farm as though Alexis were blind—the olive grove, the fields of young trellised vines. She was proud of it all. She showed him the Minoan basin their grandfather had dug up with a plow. It was huge, decorated with grape-and-coral designs, and was four thousand years old. When Alexis suggested that it belonged in a museum she told him it did very well for washing clothes.

"We have chickens, too," she said, but Alexis hated chickens and would not look at them. She asked what was wrong with chickens and he said, "That's my business."

Penelope tried to catch his eyes with the steady stare of her own, but he turned away. He was a hard one to understand or like, she thought.

Gesturing toward the ridge, he said, "You've got plenty of sheep up there. You must have a sheepdog too." But Penelope shook her head, and Alexis said, "Without a dog, I'd think they'd get lost. Or stolen."

That surprised her too. There were no thieves on Crete. "There are walls to keep them from getting lost," she said.

Within moments they were scrambling over those walls and climbing to where the olive grove thinned and the soil became rocky and strewn with brambles. Below, Aghios Miron spread out, white and thatched and very still. Penelope knew it all. The congregation of tiny ants around what seemed a drop of milk were the elders sitting at a table in the square listening to the radio. The tree called Idleness dropped its inky shade around them. Legend held that its shadow was a chunk of night broken off and that those who sat under it too long would forget forever the time of day. Her father would be there, interrupting the radio to bang on the table with a closed fist and argue against what it said.

"This is a wonderful view," said Alexis.

"Everything under the sun, we have it right here in Aghios Miron," she told him expansively.

"You're wrong, though," he said. "There's a great deal you won't see here." But when she challenged him, Alexis refused to argue.

From her hilltop, Penelope could see the White Mountains and snow-capped Ida. "Zeus lived there, you know, and if you squint your eyes you can see Heraklion, where we were yesterday, way off there." Beyond the city was the sea, blue and beating with light. Out of sight beyond that curve of water lay the mainland of Greece and Europe and all the wide world, curling back and around and up to where she stood at the center of the universe. The idea made her lightheaded.

Over the ridge was a meadow where the grass was thick and elastic. They seemed to have springs in their heels as they laughed and bounced on it. Alexis looked amazed. "I haven't laughed like that—well, not since forever," he said. Again they laughed, and sat down in the thick grass with sheep prowling about them like great caterpillars. Overhead the sky seemed a bottomless well of blue from which drenched all the perfumes of spring. Alexis said, "It's funny; sometimes I have dreams about waking up

43

on a day like this. My heart's thumping a mile a minute. Before I open my eyes I know what it is. The world's slipped upside down and if I let go of the mattress I'll fall into the sky." He jabbed at the ground with a broken stick, digging up a trench.

"What is it?" she asked softly. "We were having such a good time."

Alexis did not answer. He went on gouging with the stick until it snapped. The new, happy Alexis had had a very short life.

"You're always so gloomy, almost always, aren't you?"

"I suppose I am nowadays. It's just that when I was young, practically everything good seemed to come true. You know—you'd want something and it would happen, like in the fairy stories. But now I'm always surprised when anything good happens, like today, for instance." In an astonished voice he said, "It's such a beautiful day."

"I suppose you didn't have very good weather when you lived in Scotland."

"Scotland's a good place," said Alexis, adding after a pause, "if you're Scottish. It wasn't easy for a foreigner, I guess. My father had a business in Edinburgh but it didn't make money. He sold it and we went back to Grevena. Now my father's at Thermopylae or in prison camp, I don't know where, and my mother's probably in Alexandria. She's a nurse, you know. That leaves me."

"Were you alone in Grevena when the invasion came?"

"Yes, except for the village priest," said Alexis. He was gnawing his upper lip. "The others had run to the mountains because of the bombing but I wanted to watch the road. I thought my father might be coming back with his men. If he did, he didn't come that way."

44

"That must have been awful."

"You'll never know how awful," he said, "but let's forget it. I don't want to spoil this day by telling you things you wouldn't believe."

"Grandfather'll get you to talk. He's a regular warrior, you know."

"I don't care much for warriors," said Alexis. "And I told you I'm not going to spoil things." But the day was already being spoiled by an airplane that came from the east. "I hate chickens and planes," said Alexis. The airplane passed high overhead, propellers flashing, though the motors made no sound because of the great height. It drifted west toward the sea where a bank of heavy white clouds piled, a sudsy billow about to spill over onto Crete.

"See what I told you about the weather?" he said. "It's going to rain."

They watched the distant clouds rise above the peaks and gradually expand. A sultry wind sprang up. Sulphur-yellow lightning flashed along the horizon, where black threads of rain hung down joining sky and sea. It threatened Aghios Miron and Penelope stood and watched it come, feet planted, head lifted like a wild creature listening for danger.

"What a strange light," she said.

"Because of the rain," said Alexis.

"No, it's something else. Do you hear that roar, like horses galloping?"

"It's the rain drumming in the valley. We ought to go. This will be a bad place when the lightning comes."

"Not yet," she pleaded. A yellow crack of lightning split the sky. A bellow of thunder followed and the first cold spatter of rain fell.

"But it isn't safe here," said Alexis. He took her hand

45

and she followed, wild with excitement, as the storm wind arrived with a roar, jarring the windows of the village, whipping her skirt against her legs. With the wind came lightning and rain. Shepherds appeared from nowhere to gather in the sheep. Plowmen unyoked their oxen while the village mothers, holding their blown skirts, ran after their children.

Penelope and Alexis ran headlong down the hill where the needling drops raised a smokiness along the ground. Blown this way and that by the gusts, slipping on the wet stones, they went hand in hand to keep from falling. Alone, Penelope might have stood there in the rain. She loved it. She had no fear of the lightning, but Alexis was intent upon getting home and he would not let go of her hand.

This storm was no remote affair up in the sky; it was all around them. Weird fire bounded along the ground and Penelope, running with the homebound sheep, felt the thunder bursting inside her head. Explosion after explosion reverberated from the hillside, from the mountains where her grandfather prowled. He was the sort of man who would reach his arms up to the lightning. Even the ground trembled. It must be like war, she thought, like being bombed. Her grandfather had taught her to enjoy the thunder as he himself had enjoyed the wars of his youth. Ghost armies in the sky, he called the storms, reliving the day of glory. Could she love war less than he?

A wet rushing carpet of woolen backs pressed about them. Dozens of sheep came slipping, sliding, urged on by Emmanuel's wild yells. Shouting with laughter, he swung and bolted the gate behind them, then ran toward the house, where Katerina waited with lamp held high. "Come on, you two," he shouted at Penelope and Alexis. "No sense being out there if you can help it."

They ate early that evening while the storm battered about the house, rattling the windows. Alexis hunched over his food as though he noticed nothing else, yet he scarcely ate.

"You think Grandfather's out in the storm?" said Penelope. She imagined the old man standing on a rocky crag, the lightning all about him.

"I suspect he's in a cave somewhere," said Emmanuel, "or with some shepherd. He's getting too old for that sort of life."

"I wish he'd come home. On stormy nights he used to get out the santuri and play," said Penelope.

Emmanuel said, "I was thinking of dusting it off myself."

Outside, thunder fell like an interminable cargo of rocks plunging down an infinite chasm. Dinner was over, except for Alexis, who stirred his food.

"You should honor the food," said Katerina. "Think how long it takes to grow."

Alexis began to chew, his jaws working like weary pistons. Penelope watched him suspiciously, wondering what was wrong now. A cozy night, a good storm and her father about to entertain them with music. That was enough.

From a chest in the corner, Emmanuel extracted the santuri, a flat wooden box polished by use, inlaid with ivory and crossed with a warp of metal strings. According to Penelope no one could play the fourteen-string santuri like her father. Emmanuel disagreed, saying, "Your grandfather won his way out of a Turkish prison by playing for the Pasha. That man can play like no one, living or dead." Then he asked Alexis to choose a tune.

"I'd like 'The Butcher's Dance,'" said Penelope.

"Name a tune, Alexis," urged Emmanuel.

"Well, what about 'The Fiddler's Joy'? That's a good tune," said Alexis.

" 'The Fiddler's Joy'? Could you hum a few bars?"

Alexis named other melodies, all Scottish. At last he suggested "The Butcher's Dance." "Now *there's* a tune," said Emmanuel, who began to play slowly at first with the strings barely whispering, then faster and faster.

Penelope could have surrendered herself to the music but for Alexis, who seemed to notice only the storm. She watched his hands, kneading together like nervous little animals, his legs crossing and uncrossing. Glancing around, he stared at the window where drops ran down. Except for the rain, there was nothing to see and she sensed it was not so much the weather outside that was bothering him as a secret storm locked in his memory.

"You ought to listen to the music," she told him. "He's playing just for you."

"I know that," whispered Alexis. "It's the dampness I can't stand. Rain makes everything so clammy."

Emmanuel thumped out the old tunes, the leaping Cretan dances and the sad love songs. He played the heroic ballads with a rising cadence that mounted against the thunder. For Penelope the music had become very small, a cricket scratching behind a wall. Alexis' storm had overtaken her. Terrible sounds arose, vast bodies in collision. A stampede of iron-shod horses trampled across the sky, a desperate neighing issued from the windy night. She stared at the window confused. It was an empty mirror, but she still felt the shock of hoofs on her heart.

Penelope did not notice when the music stopped. Leaning back, the santuri in his lap, Emmanuel took a deep breath of the rain-fresh air. "Aaah!" he yawned, and his teeth showed to the molars. Again the long *"Aaah!"* with his arms flung out. Except for the smile, the great sigh and the entire posture were those of a man struck by a bullet. At this instant Alexis bolted from his seat, chair clattering, and ran cringing toward the ladder.

"What's all this?" cried Emmanuel, letting his chair bump forward.

"He's gone to bed, so let him be!" snapped Katerina.

Penelope called out, "Good night, Alexis," and half-way up the ladder he turned his face toward them. Those eyes: Penelope would never forget them.

"I didn't hear him," said Emmanuel. "Did he say good night?"

Katerina lowered her voice. "What a strange boy. Did you see his expression?"

"He saw a ghost!" said Penelope, who had been taught not to believe in spirits.

Alexis did not reappear that night. There was no sound from the loft or from the night outside. But where the storm had passed the air was heavy and damp.

Then the village threw open its doors and windows. The people stepped outside and lanterns went with them, up and down the stream beds where snails would be in thousands after the rain.

Penelope and her parents took baskets and went out. Snails were good to eat but they were slimy in the palm; the feeling shot through Penelope's body like electricity and prickled the hairs at the back of her neck.

They hunted in silence until Emmanuel asked, "How are you two getting on?"

"Alexis and me? Fine, I guess."

"But you're not sure?"

"He isn't exactly what I expected. I'd like to know

why he's so full of secrets. Something must have happened to him, Papa. I don't know what it was, but it's made him such an awful coward. Look at the way the storm frightened him."

"Don't judge him yet, Pen. We don't know him." Emmanuel scooped a snail into his basket, then added thoughtfully, "Your grandfather's likely to arrive any day. That old war horse! I wonder if he'll be good or bad for the boy?"

"Well, he'll be good for me," said Penelope, who loved Old Markos so much it might have made Emmanuel jealous, were it not that she knew he loved the old man too.

four

✲✲ ✲✲ ✲✲ ✲✲ ✲✲

Markos Metaxas—Old Markos, as he was called far and wide—was almost eighty years old. He was a living legend and the reason Penelope occasionally wished she had not been born a girl. Given one wish, she would live his life over again. There were the old stories of his youth, polished smooth now by much handling, but diamond-bright. Old Markos—remember how he fought for independence? So full of Turkish lead, the story went, they could use him for an anchor when he died. In other tales he was known as

51

the Cretan Orpheus, for he had won his way out of Turkish prison with his music, by melting the Pasha's iron heart. As long as Old Markos and men like him strode the hills, Penelope would never fear for Cretan liberty.

Now he was returning to Aghios Miron. She had heard the report carried ahead by children on flying feet: "Old Markos is back!" In her imagination she could see him marching, grand as a parade with banners. The patriarchs beneath the Tree of Idleness would try to stop him. They would make a place at their table, but Old Markos would simply raise his hand in passing. Before the chapel he might hesitate to clasp hands with the priest, Father Panagos. These two men, Penelope knew, loved their country to the verge of blasphemy. For a moment their hands might lock, hard. Then Old Markos would stride up the last hillside. Did she hear the tread of boots approaching, the wild shouts of children? Penelope rushed to the door and flung it open.

There stood the old man, grown old not as a man grows old, but as a gnarled, wind-worn tree, still straight and heavy-limbed. He embraced Penelope, crushing the wind out of her, but his eyes were on Alexis.

He took the boy's hands in his large square ones. "Grandson," he said huskily, his voice dropping almost to a whisper. Then stern and demanding, "Where'd the whiteness come from, boy? Lived under a stone all your life?"

"He's Scottish . . . there isn't any sun there," said Penelope.

"From my mother," said Alexis.

"And the skinniness too, I imagine," said Markos. "Well, you've Cretan shoulders. That's a start. Katerina's cooking will fill out the rest. That right, Katerina?" The old man did not await confirmation but said to Alexis,

"Come and hit me, boy, hard as you can, right here!" and thumped his stomach.

"If you don't mind, I'd rather not."

Markos was enthusiastic. He insisted. Reluctantly Alexis drew back his fist. "Didn't feel it," said Markos. They sparred. "Now try a left!"

Finally Markos thrust out his foot and sent Alexis sprawling. Penelope was shocked. She hadn't expected such a trick from her grandfather, but when she looked at him Markos said, "Never fight fair when it's a matter of life or death, or you'll not grow up to be an old man." He helped his grandson up, then limped to a chair.

"Did I hurt your leg? I'm terribly sorry," said Alexis.

"I'm not that brittle yet, boy."

As Penelope knew, the limp represented an old wound which Markos bore as proudly as a medal awarded for valor. In wet weather he carried a stick, though he only rested on it when he was unobserved.

The old man sat straight in his chair as if he were riding a horse. "What I want to hear about is your father, that palakari son of mine," he said. "How's he doing? Why hasn't he won the war yet?"

Penelope glanced at Alexis, who was staring at his grandfather. He appeared uncertain whether the old man were real or simply a bad dream. For Penelope the silence was agonizing. She said, "Alexis doesn't like to talk about that," but Old Markos was not to be put off.

"Well, boy, what about it?"

"My father's fine. . . . I mean, he was fine when—when I last saw him. He promised to come for me here."

"Come for you!" Old Markos' voice was a thunderclap. "He can't leave his men, boy. You know that."

Another painful pause saved by a sound from outside.

Penelope heard it first, a spade turning sod. Emmanuel went to the door and disappeared. When he returned, she knew at once something was wrong. "It's that shepherd, the old fellow," he said. "He told me he's here to die. Listen, he's digging his grave!"

Katerina replied that the shepherd was a dirty old creature who would stop at nothing to wheedle a meal. But Penelope pleaded, saying that El Greco never joked. He would lie down in the grave and die if they didn't do something.

"That El Greco you're talking about used to be a circus magician," said Old Markos. "One of his acts was being buried alive."

Outside, the digging continued.

"Please, Mother, it isn't Christian!" pleaded Penelope, for whom the shepherd had been almost a second father. From him she had heard the old tales and learned the secrets of Crete only a wandering shepherd might know, and Penelope loved him with all the fondness she had for good times past.

"Aye, let him in," said Old Markos. "I like the old fool. He's too scrawny to eat much."

At this point Katerina surrendered. "All right, we'll feed him—and bathe the smelly old thing. Don't go around saying I'm not a Christian woman. Well, go on, invite him in. Tell him he can stop undermining the house." With this she returned to her cooking, punishing the pots and pans.

Penelope and Alexis went to the door. "You'll like him, Alexis," she said. "He's almost as wonderful as Grandfather."

"Then I'm not so sure," said Alexis under his breath.

Outside, a slight figure toiled with a spade. El Greco was thin, his flesh burned to the color of smoked beef. In

that dark hide the eyes were hugely blue and rolling like mischievous moons. A tiny lamb, white as cotton, rubbed against his leg.

"Ignore me, my friends," he said. "Why should you offer bread to me?" No one as yet had offered him anything. "I'm not here to eat your good food. I'm here to perish among friends."

"You can't talk that way to me," said Penelope. She took the little man by his stick of an arm. The shepherd dropped his spade willingly. In fact, he was the first one through the door.

"Good people!" he cried with a sweeping bow to all, "I'm here to steal . . . a little of your gracious friendship. It's wonderful to see you all so well." He gave a little cough, then exclaimed, "Penny! Oh, my stars, I didn't have a good look at you out there in the dark!" He stepped back. "If I were a painter as my mother, rest her soul, wanted me to be, I'd paint you riding in a seashell with the south wind blowing on one side and the north wind on the other. . . . And Katerina!" He took her hand warmly. "I've always told my friends you're the finest cook in these thousand islands." Katerina gave him a look, as if to say: Do you really think you can get around me with that talk? Quite unabashed by this reception, the shepherd rummaged in his bag, saying, "Look here, Katerina. I've this magic scarf for you. You can have it, Katerina. You wrap it around a top hat, and abracadabra, rabbits! Or goldfish in a bowl. It's a wonderful thing to have."

"Will it help the crops or cook the food?" she said, but her mellowing tones left no doubt in Penelope's mind that El Greco was staying to supper.

The hearty meal was engulfed with much gusty smacking of lips, and Penelope had expected the shepherd to attack his plate like a starved animal. Actually he scarcely ate at all, merely sampling this or that, as though he were there only for the company. Finally he sat back with a great groan and several yawns, saying there was no doubt about who was the best cook on the island.

When the plates were cleared away the inevitable conversation began again.

"Down at the Tree of Idleness the news is black. The radio says so."

"*Ha!*" said Old Markos. "Bunch of old crows. One shot and they'd drop dead of apoplexy. I want to hear what the boy has to say. He was there."

Alexis said through clenched teeth, "I don't know anything, Grandfather, except that we're losing. There won't be any Greece left and I don't care so long as my family doesn't go with it."

"What do you mean, don't care? Every Greek has to care!" roared the old man, his eyes smoldering, his hands rolled into fists.

"Crete won't ever be defeated," said Penelope.

"If you'd been there with the planes swooping down day after day, you'd know," said Alexis. "None of you really know anything."

Old Markos was beet-red. "Of course we're going to win," he said. "In the end we always do. Didn't we drive the Italians back into Albania? Answer me that. And hold them all winter?" But that had been winter and now it was spring. Nazi armor was driving to the sea and no one was stopping it. Old Markos demanded to know why. He banged the table. If they could beat the Italians, and the Turks before, why not these Germans too?

"Because you have such a tiny old-fashioned army,"

said the shepherd. He made a gesture of helplessness. "A little army can't fight a big one."

"Why not?" bellowed Old Markos. "I'd like to know why not. We did it long ago at Thermopylae and Salamis. And I did it myself, right here!" He drove his fist down against the table. "We'll drive them back again if they get this far," he said, throwing up the broad prow of his chin. "We'll fight them from the hills and in the mountains, the way we did with the Turks." His eyes glistened with remembrance.

Certainly they would fight. Penelope had no doubts. She could imagine no reluctance among the others. Perhaps Alexis was too much of a coward, but the rest would stand together. Believing this, it came as a surprise when El Greco said, "Will you listen to that old man? When I hear talk like that I can't believe the world's as old as scientists say, since it can't be many generations since our ancestors slithered out of the sea. If every old corpse like yourself takes out every rusty blunderbuss in town and marches off to the mountains, what difference will it make? This is a war for great armies, millions of machines, not a few peasants who can only make it harder for themselves and their relatives. The Nazis will come here for the naval base and the airfield. Believe me, they wish the peasants no harm. This dreaming of the old days makes me sad."

"If I didn't know you were a doddering old fool," said Markos, "I'd call you a traitor."

Penelope looked from one to the other. She was confused, feeling her grandfather must be right, but wondering how the little shepherd, a man she had always considered so very wise, could be completely wrong.

"Alexis, listen to me," said Old Markos. "You're a boy with strange ideas. Maybe that's because you come from a strange country, I don't know. But this is Crete, and it belongs to us and always will. We've been invaded before. The Romans came, the Venetians, and the Turks. These Nazis will come and take it all, unless we stop them the way we finally stopped the Turks. Lord, we were fighters then! Oh, yes, we were something to watch in the old days."

"No stories," said El Greco. "I can see the light in his eyes. Those days won't come back. Let them rest." But Penelope liked her grandfather's stories, and the old man intended to tell them, not to brag as this fool of a shepherd might think, but to show his grandson that the words *Crete* and *liberty* were inseparable.

"Yes, tell how it was—for Alexis," said Penelope.

Alexis was silent, but El Greco added, "Prepare yourself, Alexis. Your grandpa killed more Turks than the Black Plague. He killed more than the Grim Reaper. Let him tell you all about it."

The old warrior began to talk. For Markos, history began on Black Tuesday in 1453 when Sultan Fatin Mehmet marched over the walls of Constantinople and the Turkish Night began. The hard old lips moved, the fierce old eyes were unblinking. "It wasn't until years later they came to Crete, and then it took them twenty years to break the walls of Heraklion. Twenty years, boy, of cannons, smoke and hunger."

"This was before your grandpa's time, Alexis," said the shepherd, "but there was some gaunt old man just like him howling about patriotism and telling his boys to march out and fight."

"Hush, let him tell it," said Penelope.

The story went on. "My father fought in two revolutions. He was at the Arkadion monastery when the Turks hemmed them in and hope ran out. You've heard how the abbot touched a torch to the powder magazine and the whole garrison rode to heaven in a fiery chariot. My father was destroyed all right, but he was never defeated. That's what I want you to understand, boy.

"I was just your age, Alexis, when the last revolution came long. We'd been crushed in six, seven, I don't know how many revolutions, but we weren't defeated. My grandfather was an old man then, and I was a boy, but we marched into the hills to melt down the lead from church roofs into bullets, while the Turks came for us with their reserves. Have you ever seen Dervishes, boy? No? They're a fearful sight, let me tell you, with their green skirts and pointed hats. And when they come at you they bark like dogs, like a pack of howling dogs gone mad. We stood our ground, boy, and we can again."

Of all the old stories, this was Penelope's favorite. It rang in her ears like the sounding of a trumpet.

"That's how I took this wound. Look here, boy," and Markos rolled up his left pant leg, revealing a white-ridged scar, which Penelope as a child had touched with her finger. She had giggled then, not knowing why, but she did not do so now. She wondered how it must have felt in those first blinding seconds, and the story did not sound as glorious as it had.

"He paid for it, I'll tell you, with both his ears. We took souvenirs in those days. I kept a bottle full of pickled ears, though I'm not so proud of the collection as I used to be. . . ."

"After all," interjected the shepherd, "it isn't convenient when you make friends with people later on and invite them home, for their ears to be there before they arrive."

Alexis was staring at his plate. "That," he finally managed without looking up, "is horrible!" From his expression there might have been a half-devoured bug on the plate. "I presume that's what happened to the blacksmith. You have his ear?"

Old Markos was silent. "Yes," he said finally. "I've often felt badly about that. But it hasn't stopped us being friends."

Alexis shuddered. He was holding on very tightly to the seat of his chair. He certainly was not much of a boy, thought Penelope. It wasn't as though anyone were hacking at *his* ears. The Turk and her grandfather were blood brothers now; what more could he want?

"Well," said Markos, getting back to his story, "we were up there in the mountains, winter coming on and we didn't expect any help. Still, we fought like lions."

"Strange," said El Greco. "Among lions, it's the females are the fighters."

"Stop making fun! Are you calling me a liar?" roared Markos, shoving his chair back and starting to rise.

"Heaven forbid! I meant only that you fought like female lions."

Markos sat back again. "We had resigned ourselves to die rather than surrender; then at the last, Greece came to her senses. Prince George came with the fleet and the Turks surrendered without a fight. All I want to tell you is this, boy. When those ships steamed in, decked out in flags, and the Prince set foot on Cretan soil, we were liberated. Have you ever seen a whole people gone wild because they've just seen freedom for the first time? I guess not. Well, then, you'll always be just a little bit blind. It's something I can't explain. You'd have to be there yourself to understand."

"Tell the boy how different freedom was, how the grain grew twice as high in the fields, how the wine was so much sweeter because the Turks had gone," said El Greco.

"What if the new wine was bitter? It was our wine, and the grain was our grain, and it was our glory. And when you and I are long forgotten, Greeks will remember how we marched to glory, how we fought in those days. Lord, I can see myself stepping off behind the drums, silver pistols in my belt——" He gazed upward into the smoky candlelight and seemed to see it all. "Emmanuel," he said, "you've got my revolvers somewhere. Has Alexis seen them?"

"No!" said Alexis and Emmanuel more or less together, both with consternation.

"Well, let's have them out here on the table. It's time to talk of guns."

"Frankly, sir," said Alexis, "I'm not fond of guns."

"A grandson of mine? We'll soon change that. Get the guns, Emmanuel!" Emmanuel went reluctantly; Penelope knew he had long since buried the weapons at Katerina's insistence.

"So you don't like guns, eh? Do you love your country, boy?"

Alexis said nothing, but settled in his chair, assuming the shrunken posture Penelope had come to expect in moments of stress. She did not know what thoughts darted through his mind; he would not tell and she no longer cared. In a moment he would undoubtedly dash from the room.

"You've a lifetime to sit still, boy, and hold your tongue. But now you're conversing with me, your grandfather. At least I'm speaking to you. Everyone loves his country. Everyone's patriotic."

"I'm nothing," said Alexis. "I only wish you would leave me alone." Penelope opened her eyes wide. She had never heard such a despairing voice. And what Old Markos might have said, no one would know, for Emmanuel en-

61

tered with the guns, blackly tarnished, far from the bright destroyers Markos had pictured.

"Good Lord! My guns?" He picked them up, let the hammers fall. "Well, they still work and that's what matters." Shoving the guns across the table toward Alexis, he added, "It takes a good man to pull those triggers. Try it." Alexis refused to touch them. The evening was an ordeal for him.

"Let him be," said the shepherd. "Pick on me if you like."

Old Markos said, "I never pick on anyone smaller than myself and I'm not concerned with driving frightened puppies into battle. We need men with courage who love their country and are ready to fight. I'm speaking of Emmanuel. He's the one to organize the villagers." They looked at the old man, nonplused. "Naturally; who's more respected here?"

All this time Emmanuel had kept his own counsel, but now he would have to speak out. Penelope waited breathless, sure that he shared his father's defiant spirit, wondering only what words he would choose. Would he speak as a poet, the way he spoke of spring?

"Perhaps the time for that sort of fighting is over," said Emmanuel calmly.

"I only said 'perhaps,'" he cautioned, as Markos ground his teeth and Penelope stared. "Alexis, now, has been there. He's seen these new weapons. Men can only do so much with their bare hands. Perhaps it's all up to the great armies now."

"But Papa, are you saying we should run away?" said Penelope, her voice shrill with disbelief.

"I don't know what I'm saying," said Emmanuel. "Perhaps a man belongs in the army, not on his own. We'll have to wait and pray and when the time comes, make our own decisions."

"There's only one decision . . . *fight!* Look at this house; the best in town. You don't think you'll go on quietly farming, do you? They'll take everything if you permit them to and leave you beggars in the street."

Penelope knew Old Markos was right. There was no other answer.

"I'd rather be a beggar than kill a man," said Alexis.

"You!" said Old Markos, nothing more, but the single word bore all the venom of an inquisitor pronouncing sentence. Doggedly Alexis persisted; he would never fire a gun. What a queer cousin she had, thought Penelope. He was as conspicuous a coward as she had ever met, and yet he had the pluck to contradict Markos, a thing few men would dare.

"I wish," said El Greco, "that war was as simple as you people make it sound: fight until it gets dark, get a good night's sleep, in the morning have a victory parade. If God had intended us to fight, He'd have given us horns and claws. If we all simply do as we always have, stay on our farms, tend our flocks, things needn't change. They may not even bother with this little town. It's when farmers hide in caves with homemade bombs that innocent people get shot and children starve."

"That's enough!" Markos crashed the pistols down on the table. "I never said war wasn't a dreadful thing, but it is also a splendid thing. When war comes to Crete she will meet it as she would the Angel Gabriel!" He dared contradiction.

Alexis had turned in his chair. Penelope wanted to turn him back forcibly, make him fight for what he believed. Even though Old Markos was right in what he said, she did not like to see him browbeating such a weak opponent. Someone should say something, but Alexis was obviously silenced and she could not oppose her beloved grandfather. In the end, it was the shepherd who refused to be cowed. "Go on. Destroy everything, mutilate the people, cut out their dreams and their poor frightened souls. You insane, unholy maniacs!" This was too strong, thought Penelope. It was the shepherd who was beginning to sound like a maniac. "It doesn't matter," continued El Greco. "There will always be flocks on the hilltops and shepherds watching them."

"Ha! Listen to him. El Greco thinks he's a poet but he's just a parrot. Look out, if we don't keep him in a cage he'll peck our eyes out." There was no good will in Marko's mockery.

"That's enough, Markos. Let him alone," said Emmanuel.

"The trouble with all of you," Old Markos shouted, "you don't want things hard enough."

"Don't you mean loud enough?" This from Alexis. A deadly hush followed. Penelope half-expected to see lightning flash between them. The old man rose, looming over the table; then he composed himself and sat down, drumming his fingers on the knee that was grooved with battle wounds. "That boy is no grandson of mine," he said. "He belongs in the same cage with that parrot there." Then he laughed and rocked back in his chair, clicking the pistols—one, two, three times.

"You ignorant, ignorant old man!" shouted Alexis in a voice choked with angry tears.

Penelope sat with her hand covering the lower part of her face, too aghast to condemn or applaud either one.

"No cowards in Crete!" bellowed Old Markos.

Alexis scrambled to his feet. Emmanuel leaped up, taking his father's arm. "Markos, he's only a boy." Markos shook off the grasp and shouted again, *"No cowards in Crete!"* His right hand was raised and his fist was closed around an imaginary stick.

Alexis turned from the table, upsetting a glass, which rolled icily across the floor. He went to the door and snatched the coat hanging there. Penelope watched him, spellbound with amazement as his arm caught in the sleeve of the heavy garment that seemed about to wrestle him to the floor. He grabbed at the door and pulled it open. Then Alexis was gone. El Greco, excusing himself, followed.

So the party ended abruptly. Penelope would never forget it. She would never mention the dispute to either Old Markos or Alexis, though she was aware of a guilty silence between the two thereafter. The only tangible evidence of their first encounter was the two black guns which had come out of the ground and would never be reburied.

five

♈ ♈ ♈ ♈ ♈

During those late spring days there was much to worry about in Aghios Miron. There was the weather. The spring rains had held off and day after day the skies were clear. At night the stars drooped lower, like cruel unfriendly flowers. There was not enough water in the wells to keep the fields from cracking and drying out. There was also the war. This too was a problem for the peasant farmers, though still a distant one, brought to them over a few small radios. All day the village elders sat under the Tree of

Idleness listening to the radio and sipping thick black coffee, though soon there would be no more coffee and none coming to Crete. Old Markos listened, and told them to look to their guns. He went from house to house speaking to the men, and on his hips as he limped through the streets were his revolvers.

In the Metaxas house there was another worry, that of a fiery old man and a grandson who did not love one another. They kept a smoldering distance, straining those ties of family loyalty which among Greeks are the strongest bonds. Fortunately, the warm dry weather kept them apart, Markos spending his days in the village recruiting while Alexis worked beside his uncle in the fields. Penelope found herself estranged from both, unable to side with either. Years of love and loyalty bound her to Old Markos, yet her sympathy was with Alexis. He had been robbed of his own family and seemed so completely defenseless. Thus Penelope, a girl who seldom wasted time on deep thought, argued with herself and, when released from work in the fields or house, took longer and lonelier walks than she ever had before. From the hills above town, her world and the problems it contained seemed smaller. Far below, the sun made white winks on Emmanuel's hoe as it rose and fell. Her family toiled in the dust, turning over their land to the sun. Sometimes their hoes unearthed bits of white-washed stone, fragments of pottery. For centuries past houses had stood here, now returned to the earth along with the men and women who had lived in them. So their farm would one day return to the soil, with their bodies and those of their children. Each man and woman had his turn at drawing life from the soil. With buckets of water they tried to revive the thirsting earth under their feet as their ancestors had done through the ages. Yes, the quarrels of a boy and his grandfather seemed very small from the hills.

On one such stroll she encountered the shepherd. El Greco was lounging on a boulder and seemed not the least surprised to see her. "I've been waiting for you here," he said.

"What made you think . . . ? I've never been to this spot before in my life."

El Greco tapped his forehead as one might tap the shell of an egg. "We magicians. . . . And I know another thing. You've got a problem."

"How do you know that?"

"Let's say because of the way you were walking. It doesn't matter why I can tell. It's that dragon of a grandfather and the boy," said El Greco. "I feel very sorry for Alexis."

"That's because he agrees with you," said Penelope.

"Yes, partly, but he's gone through an awful lot, things that shouldn't happen to a living soul. Take my word for it."

"Then he must have told you what happened to him," said Penelope. "He wouldn't tell me but he told you the other night after the argument."

"Supposing he did," said El Greco. "He'll tell you himself, in time, when you can understand. It's not up to me."

"Well," said Penelope, "why should I care if you have secrets?" From her tone she obviously cared very much. "Whatever it is, I think you're both wrong. I don't know much about war, but we're not letting anyone come here and take our farm."

"What makes me sad is that you're both right, really."

"That's impossible," said Penelope.

"I wouldn't want to have you angry with an old

friend," said El Greco, "but when you've lived as long as I, you won't be quite so sure of what's right or wrong."

"You're not so old, not as old as Grandfather," she said.

"You'd be surprised if I told you. Yes, you'd be surprised how long my people have lived in Crete. See the tree by the wall with the gnarled trunk? That's an old tree, say a thousand years, but my people were here long before that tree was a seed, three generations of trees like that, more than that by far. Long before the Minoans, I was here."

"You mean your ancestors?" asked Penelope.

"Hush!" said the shepherd. "You know I'm a magician and tell nothing but lies. Oh, you should have seen this island then. What a dragon she was, with palaces on every hilltop laid down like rusty dragon eggs. King Minos reigned and his navies swept the seas. They said the empire would never die, but it all went up in smoke."

"I know the story of Icarus," said Penelope, "how he fell into the sea."

"Like a shooting star," said El Greco. "Crete's first air casualty. I wish I could say he was the last, but we've seen lots of changes between then and now."

"Who's we?"

"Why, myself and Crete. You Greeks showed up and finished off the Minoans, took their farms away from them, by the way. I wonder if the Minoans had any old warriors like your grandfather, or any girls like you. No matter, you Greeks have been here too long to worry over the feelings of Minoans. There've been others, too. Romans. They left their statues and disappeared, but before they left they were in charge for a thousand years. You didn't like them much; you weren't free, but they left you good roads and your church. Those were troublesome times to live through," said El Greco.

"But you were here, all along, tending your sheep," said Penelope, slipping into the fantasy.

"Yes, that's about right," said the shepherd, "up here tending my sheep and believing one minute the Minoans were right, and then the Greeks. I was beginning to wonder whether, with things so confusing, if it wasn't about time for me to be getting home."

"Home? Where? This is home."

El Greco said, "I told you, my people came from another island; but I kept hanging around watching the Turks putting up their minarets when they got the upper hand and then watching you Greeks pull them down again. Your grandfather believes the Turks were wrong. He's still angry about them, but it's hard to be angry or sure of anything when you look back over thousands of years."

"But what's important is right now," said Penelope, "and besides, you're just giving me a history lesson. What's that got to do with you?"

"Oh, you know about the old carnival trickster, doing magic that looked so real that people couldn't tell the difference between what was genuine and what was fake. When it got so I wasn't sure myself, that was time to get back to my sheep. That's my story, part of it, Pen. What about you—all sugar and spice like the story goes?"

"I guess I'm made up of two things," said Penelope. "My mother and father equally, but that isn't any help when I try to think about Alexis and Grandfather. My parents haven't said much. Papa thinks I should try to get along with both of them. They don't say who's right, but when the time comes, they'll stay and fight. I know they will. If you could only see the way they love the farm, and I do, too."

"Of course you do," said the shepherd. "It couldn't be any other way."

"But if they come, what about you? You're not a fighter. You wouldn't pretend to bury yourself like you did the other night."

"No, no cheap carnival tricks," said El Greco. "Don't you think an old haunted castle like me ought to be torn down or buried, without any tricks?"

"Promise me you won't bury yourself or disappear," she pleaded.

El Greco placed two fingers on the girl's wrist, in the manner of a blind man. "There are still a few things that need doing," he assured her, "and you'll know, when the time comes. For a person like me, not being sure what's really right and really wrong, it's hard to know when to die. I don't intend to end up in a shallow ditch in your back yard, though. No, when I go home it will be an evening like this, but with lightning flickering on the horizon. Then I'll fly away on wings so delicate and fine they'll have only ghost colors like an oil slick on dark water. You'll never see me passing against the blue sky."

"But when it's storming?"

"Why, then, I'll fly above the clouds and the wind will keep me up. At night I'll spread those great wings out on the wind and sleep."

"I wish you had an extra set of wings like that," said Penelope.

"I wish I had, Pen, for you, but they aren't made any more."

Then the shepherd pointed off toward the west where fleecy clouds edged with gold drifted slowly across the

71

darkening lavender sky, looking like ships one moment, like swans the next, dappled and seaborne, voyaging north-west on the wind. "Look there," he said. "It's like a vision."

At first she saw only the sunset. Then, following the clouds, so far above that their trumpeting sounded like unearthly conversation, flew the cranes, their endless battalions ranging across the heavens. Borne on the Cucumber Wind, they flew on toward Europe.

Below in the fields, Alexis and Katerina stooped to their work with complete absorption, but Emmanuel had put aside his hoe and was shielding his eyes. Then he pointed them out to his wife, these heralds of summer, bursting up from the rainforests of Africa, bringing the good season.

Penelope saw all this from the hill and sensed her parents' joy and wonder at the great birds which passed with a rushing sound, their feathers whirling like bright metal in the evening light. Suddenly when the birds soared directly overhead, Alexis looked up. As Penelope observed him from afar, the boy appeared to go mad. He ran wildly, trampling through the furrows, fell, ran again, and finally threw himself face down in the dust, without apparent reason. Then he lay still with his head cradled in his arms until the cranes had disappeared. She saw Emmanuel go to the fallen figure and help him up. How could she possibly understand, not sharing Alexis' background and the shocks which composed it? Even his later explanation seemed inadequate, that what he had seen were not the cranes, but a memory of dive bombers plummeting down the mountain valleys of Greece.

"So that's what's been bothering you all along. Why do you keep a thing like that secret?" she asked him, but he only looked at her, smiled sadly, and told her she was wrong. Beyond this he would not enlarge, nor did Penelope press him to expose his depressing memories. Better to think of the cranes with which her spirits soared. She felt their wild freedom like a breath of pure oxygen. There were so many stories about the cranes. El Greco had said that they carried swallows on their wings and in the deep hollows of their bodies. No one had ever been close enough to say it wasn't true. Harder still to believe was his tale of the cranes and the pygmies, a story which he said came from an old acquaintance of his named Plato, who believed the cranes flew north from an ageless war in the forests of Africa. There, goat-straddling pygmies waited in ambush with poison-tipped arrows. All summer long, the cranes lived in the north, then with the autumn days they returned to battle. The armies were so well matched there could be no final victory. They fought without beginning or end, an eternal war.

six

𝖂𝖂𝖂𝖂𝖂

Holy Week 1941: the bells of Aghios Miron pealed and it was like hearing the voices of ancestors, so old were the bells. In other parts of Greece the church bells were silent, drowned by the din of war. But for Penelope, standing on the hillside, they rang joyously within her, on a level with her heart.

Below her, Aghios Miron began to smoke and to smell of charcoal and hot loaves. The whole town baked. Then, when the week was done, it would open its mouth and swallow the bread and the roast lamb of the Easter feast.

Many were the rituals of Holy Week. The women of Aghios Miron cleaned their chapel and old Job the burro was enlisted. With Penelope leading, he slouched sleepily back and forth with garlands of jasmine, wreaths of camomile, basil and marjoram. Where space remained women hung aprons of calico and silk which they dedicated to the Holy Mother. Spring brides brought the finest, embroidered with words of praise to the Virgin.

On Thursday occurred the procession of the sacred icon, so strong in curative powers that every bed in town was occupied the night before and many pilgrims slept in the streets and the courtyard of the chapel. For the procession, the street was packed with people kneeling or lying in the street awaiting the priests with the holy icon of Aghios Miron to bless them. Penelope and Katerina knelt at the end of the line and before the procession appeared others had extended the column out of sight around the corner. Far off there appeared a glitter of scarlet and white. A close procession of priests and choirboys moved down the streets toward the chapel and as the sacred image passed people crossed themselves and bowed their heads. Soldiers bore the holy icon on a litter. When the litter passed, Penelope closed her eyes and prayed, for herself, for her family, for Crete, for everything she loved, and in the end she prayed for Alexis, too.

In this way, the Thursday before Easter began. It ended in quite another fashion, with the stoning of Judas Iscariot. This occurred at night and Penelope loved it. She had always gone with her grandfather, but since he was not home she persuaded Alexis. Torches flickered throughout the town as they walked, through mysterious fluttering light and wandering shadows, giving fearsome features to the ordinary. As though through a crack in time itself, scenes leapt forward from an era when witches were burned alive.

Outside the church was a straw dummy of Judas, already tattered by the rocks when they arrived. "Pick up any stone you can find," she told him. Alexis stared about bewildered. Penelope hurled a stone at the straw figure as the others were doing. When it finally toppled over, a man trotted from the crowd, waving his arms overhead. The stoning stopped and the man placed the dummy upright on a heap of sticks and brambles. He ran back to the bellowing throng and the rocks rained down. "Come on, throw," said Penelope, but Alexis had thrust his hands into his pockets. "What's the matter?" she asked him.

Alexis whispered, "Just look at their faces."

"So?" They were faces of neighbors and friends.

"They're all furious. How can they hate a pile of straw?" It was true. Many of the faces were contorted with rage. They hurled rocks as though they stoned a living enemy. Penelope had never noticed this before. How would her own face look in a mirror? The dummy was disintegrating under the stones. One of the men lunged forward with a torch, then others. When they fell back, the pyre was blazing and Judas sprawled on the top, a flaming wooden skeleton.

"You certainly can spoil just about anything," she said bitterly.

By the bright glare of the burning Judas they found their way home, Alexis silent and thoughtful, Penelope silent and provoked, for she knew in her heart she could never again enjoy this part of Easter. Surely they could not be angry with a straw dummy. This was simply a game. How then would their faces look if a living enemy twisted on the flaming pyre?

Easter Sunday arrived with chapel chimes that began at dawn and would continue all day and into the night. The villagers bathed in hoarded water and dressed in their finest petticoats and softest boots for this most important day of the year. Then it was waiting all morning and all afternoon, fasting until that moment in the evening when the shout went up from hundreds of throats: "He is risen!"

Penelope dressed in velvet bodice and red-trimmed apron over many petticoats, an annual vanity in which she delighted. She knew her mother would wear a similar outfit and Emmanuel would be turned out in red-lined cloak with a twist of scarf on his head. He would look like a handsome stage villain. She realized sadly that Alexis would have only his old rumpled suit. Her grandfather had the traditional garb if he chose to wear it, but he had stated that he would make no concession to Easter. The Greeks, he had said, should look to their ramparts, and he would wear his usual baggy black. This seemed unnecessarily stern to Penelope, but she accepted Old Markos as a creature of principle. In the end, he not only wore black but both pistols sprouting from his belt. They gleamed darkly with the sheen of old silver and oil, and inappropriate as they might seem for Easter, no one dared suggest he leave them at home.

Musicians with pipes and harps milled in the growing crowd. Their threads of thin and happy music went in at the windows, pried open the doors and the villagers came outside and followed the band.

"Rings and combs! Glass mirrors! Saint Meno in natural colors! Prayer candles!" hawked a seller of gimcracks.

Alexis fished in his pocket. "Here's for a Saint Meno."

He gave it to Penelope as an Easter gift. She didn't know how to thank him. She didn't deserve it, not from Alexis.

The church and the area round about were crowded. Penelope carried a long candle, as did many others. She strained to see. The priest was climbing to the platform before the church. He had been the village priest as long as she could remember and whenever she thought of the word *priest,* a slight figure with feathery hair and two pearly white hands came to mind: Father Panagos, *Papa Panagos* as he was called in Greek. Imprisoned in yards of rich brocade she recognized a devoted soul. His priesthood had given him stature and he had given it humanity. Now Penelope and the others waited for his words on the darkest Easter in memory.

Penelope looked down at her hands. They were stained red.

"Cut yourself?" whispered Alexis.

"This statue seems to have marked me."

Father Panagos heaved open the great Gospel, grappled elbow-deep in the trials of David and Saul. The crowd listened, their faces turned up, but Penelope rubbed her stained hands and Old Markos shifted on his feet and muttered to his neighbor. He was not interested in the kingdom of heaven. His concern was earth, and not all of that. The enemy was trampling their beloved country into the dust. This was no time for sermons.

Penelope and Alexis huddled over the little figure of Meno. Alexis said, "The heat from your hands must have done something to the paint. Throw it away." But Penelope insisted she liked the little figure and whispered, "It was really nice of you. I mean it."

Father Panagos had closed the Bible. Penelope realized he was through with the scriptures. He would speak now of Greece in her ancient glory and Greece as she was today. His words she would trust for they would come from an honest heart, though she had heard gossip that Papa Panagos was too patriotic to be a true man of God. This was the talk of old women and Penelope thought it correct for a priest to love his country. Hadn't the priests of old led their people firmly in war, as they had in peace? Without such leaders Greece would no longer exist. There was nothing unusual in the speech's beginning. Despite the heroic resistance of the Greek army, they were losing. Must they constantly be reminded? Yet the crowd had grown so still, the priest's voice so loud, one had to listen. "The fight for Greece is almost over," he said. "I fear the battle for Crete is about to begin." The people stirred. Father Panagos went on to tell them that the government was fleeing the mainland and that the national treasury of gold bars was being brought to Crete. "It must never fall into the hands of the enemy."

Penelope whispered, "Can you imagine, Alexis? All that gold! Forty-two tons of it!"

"No, I can't, and I apologize for that six-drachma plaster saint. He's spoiling your scarf."

"Hush," said Penelope. "He's nice, but I want to hear Papa Panagos."

From a distance the priest's eyes seemed to be closed but his voice was loud, a torrent of words that sent a chill down Penelope's back. It was as though he called to them from a trance, not in his own voice, but with a greater one from beyond the world. She could not know, standing there amid the enraptured crowd, that for what he was about to say, the priest would spend the next nights before the altar, asking God's pardon.

"It is a glorious thing to see arms in the hands of Greeks. We must acquaint ourselves with the sight of arms, and the use of them." The words flowed from his lungs in a rushing torrent. The crowd was electrified. "There are more terrible things than bloodshed and one of them is slavery!" His voice was as shrill and demanding as the whine of a bullet.

"That's a regular captain of a priest," exclaimed Markos, brandishing his pistols on high. "He's the one to lead us. Father Panagos to lead us!" The shout was repeated by others, some shouting "Old Markos!" until the two names were blended.

"I will no longer call you my parishioners, but comrade soldiers!" shouted the priest, his mouth so wide that the torchlight flickered on his palate. Not until he stood alone in the chapel before the icon of Christ would he have doubts.

"Papa Panagos! . . . Old Markos! . . . these to lead us!" The shouts went up into the darkness, frightening pigeons from the bell tower. The bells rang as Old Markos was shoved forward to join the priest on the platform.

Penelope felt her heart beat faster, threatening to burst her chest. Her grandfather's glory was her own. "If they come here we will greet them with bloody hands, and welcome them with open graves," a voice boomed over the crowd. Old Markos? The priest? She could not tell; it was the voice of all Cretans. A warrior of flint and pitch swelled in every breast; Alexis alone was mute and uncheering.

"Now what ails you, Alexis?" Penelope demanded.

"Their faces," he said.

"What about their faces?" she challenged him. "They love their country; we all do. What about their faces?" It did not occur to her then, or later, that he meant these faces were those which had gazed on Judas, filled not with love of country but with unreasoning hatred.

Finally Father Panagos reopened the Bible and read about the resurrection of Christ, and the words he read were silver words and his voice reverberated not as it had before, but like a silver bell when it is struck. Then he closed the book and shouted so that all would hear, "Christ is risen!"

Old Markos raised his gun and cheered.

"Christ is risen! Christ is risen!" echoed back the many throats.

Hundreds of candles were lit, firecrackers began going off in the air, underfoot. Gradually the throng of villagers thinned out, homeward bound to the waiting banquets. Throughout dinner, there were short dull explosions and skyrockets opened high overhead like bright blooming flowers.

Their stomachs full of roast lamb, Penelope and Alexis went outside to watch.

"What I can't get over," said Penelope, "is the gold. Can you imagine all that gold?" Neither could picture such a treasure, nor was there any reason to suspect that within a very few days they would be sleeping in the midst of it.

Emmanuel, the santuri under his arm, joined them. Penelope slipped her arm through his. Together they went down to the village where dancing had begun. It seemed good to have such a carefree father, such a famous grandfather. Everything seemed good to Penelope on this Easter night. This was the way it always should be. If it weren't for Alexis: he alone was disturbing, as though war, that other world from which he came, had left an ugly desolate smell upon his clothing. The boy was with them now. It wasn't his fault that he'd been hurt, had his ideas twisted out of shape. Smiling, she clasped his hand.

The Metaxas farm was left empty. Somewhere a shepherd's dog barked. A soft piping arose high in the hills. Down below, the lively Easter bells rang on and before long there came the windborne strumming of a santuri. Easter was coming to an end.

seven

The days were longer now,
and the dry wind had
parched the first green flush of spring. Summer would
come as it did each year, but there would be a difference.
There was always that crowd around the Tree of Idleness,
listening to the radio. Old Markos was no longer the only
man with guns. In the cool of evening they drilled in the
market square, the old men and the boys. The young men
had long since left, fighting hopeless battles on the mainland.
There was talk of their being evacuated back to Crete, but

no one knew. There were no letters, no news of sons and cousins and brothers. The government had fled from Athens to the safety of Egypt, and the swastika now flew above the Acropolis.

Penelope watched the drilling. She thought they looked splendid, though a passing stranger might have wondered if their arsenal had been stolen from a museum. Their women, and the men too old even to march, watched them from doorways.

But the warm laughing days of the Cucumber Wind were made for happiness. May was the month of weddings and picnics, a good month always. It began with the drubbing of a drum and a barbed-wire voice crying from a gypsy throat, "Pictures, color pictures!"

Every year the gypsies came with their pictures of famous cities. They came to sing and dance and tell the most wonderful lies. Some said the gypsies with their dark faces and tragic eyes could conjure Satan out of hell. There was no need of Satan now; they were here for a wedding.

Penelope packed a May Day picnic basket. If time were running out for Aghios Miron and a small voice hissed in her ear "This is the last, this is the last," she did not listen. Like everyone else she drowned her fears in gaiety.

"Let's go, Alexis," she called. "Picnic's ready. Let's have our fortunes told by the gypsy parrot."

Swingingly, they bore the basket between them.

On the corner, they found the gypsy photographer. Little children called him the color-picture man because he sold post cards as well. In years past, a green parrot had paced the top of his wooden camera, picking paper fortunes out of a cup.

"Where's the parrot?" asked Penelope.

"That was one old bird," cackled the gypsy. "On his last legs, ha, ha, ha!"

"But where is he?"

"He was a fancy-pants parrot," said the gypsy. "Green coat, red vest, ha, ha, ha! What feathers! What a fortune teller!"

"Yes, but what happened?" persisted Penelope.

"Why, one day he turned up a card, said it's too hot for an ancient parrot like you. Ha, ha, ha, he read his own fortune! No fortune today, the parrot's joined his ancestors. None of you kids got any futures, ha, ha, ha!"

Penelope and Alexis edged through the crowd. The gypsy was still laughing, and they did not discuss him or his parrot. The entire affair seemed ill-omened.

They took a path into the fields. Alexis said he had once had a pack of Tarot cards. He had enjoyed reading the future.

"What else do you like to do, Alexis?" She really knew so little about him.

"Well, lots of things; say, going on picnics."

"No, I mean, what would you like to be?"

"My mother wanted me to play the bagpipes. Honestly. Sounds like a joke, doesn't it?"

"What's wrong with bagpipes?"

Alexis said, "I don't mean the little ones you have here. I mean the Scottish pipes. I don't know. I guess I couldn't stand the case. All packed away it looked like a coffin for a baby."

"Well," said Penelope, "you never know the truth about people."

"Not if you're lucky."

"Is the truth about you really so dreadful, Alexis? You say very little about yourself."

"I never lie," said Alexis.

"No, because we scarcely talk at all. Is it because of the bombing? Anyone could be upset by that."

"I really don't want to discuss it," said Alexis.

"But it's best to talk about things and not keep them bottled up," said Penelope.

"All right," said Alexis, his voice so flat he might have been reading from a chart. "The bombing. We were bombed every day for so many days I can't remember. It was like the sun suddenly falling down and bursting in the street. The first time I was at home, and there was a wagon train of oxen going to the front and another one coming back. If you knew my town you'd know oxen have a hard time passing, the road is so narrow, but they were trying to get by when the planes came. There wasn't anything glorious or brave about it, whatever Grandfather thinks. The soldiers ran. They never came back and there were hardly any oxen left, all killed and torn apart in the street. Everyone left town; it was too horrible to stay there. Then we were bombed on the road and every time I lay flat on my face so frightened I could hardly breathe. But I was lucky, anyway. There are a lot worse things than being bombed."

"But what, Alexis? What could be worse? That's what you ought to get off your mind."

"No, let's leave it." A look of weariness came into his face. His hands brushed over his eyes. "There's nothing to do about it now."

"But Alexis. . . ."

"Besides," he interrupted, "there's something out there." He pointed toward the sea, shrouded in morning mist, where vague shapes, silent and ghostly, were stirring.

"You ought to know the fishing fleet comes home this time of day."

"But Penny, they haven't dared go out for weeks."

"Maybe last night they dared, or maybe it's the shadows of little clouds on the water, Alexis. You know how they look. Or maybe it's even the forty-two tons of gold Papa Panagos was talking about." But Alexis assured her that even forty-two tons of gold would not require more than one ship.

"Well, right now there isn't any way we can find out, or anything that we could do about it if we did find out, is there?" said Penelope. She gave Alexis a sly sideways glance, then dropped her handle of the basket and ran gaily, weaving between brambles and stones until she vanished behind a huge gray block of stone. Alexis followed.

"What gets into you, anyway?" he gasped.

"Don't you know? Sometimes you start running and

something dreadful

"Well, this place

," said Penelope,

r lunch on the hot

and they ate it in

ighing so that they

aid Penelope.

k of people going

hot there. I mean,

ey're down there,

ir pictures taken."

been unknown in his country.

mphasized the realistic

Rembrandt portrayed them

interesting light effects

the prosaic Dutch people.

members of his family.

showy in dress and pose.

d more serious.

s, Rembrand

"And listening to the radio, and marching around in circles like a bunch of grenadiers."

"Not on May Day," said Penelope.

"Ha!" said Alexis. "You don't know your own grandfather. He's probably got them digging trenches now."

"You shouldn't talk that way. He's your grandfather, too, and he's just trying to do the right thing."

"I can't help it," said Alexis. "One kind of person I can't stand is the kind who has the best intentions for everybody and manages to get them killed."

"Alexis, that's not fair. Our grandfather didn't start this war. He hasn't gotten anyone killed."

"He will, but that's not the point. I'm not just talking about him. I'm talking about anyone who thinks he has a right to get other people involved. Maybe I just don't like crowds any more."

"And maybe I don't like you very much," said Penelope, "but people have to get along. We're not hermits."

"Thanks. Would you like me to stop eating your picnic?" said Alexis.

It was at this point that El Greco made his presence known. How long he had been there, sitting quietly on a boulder with his hands clasped about his knees, they did not know. "Hey, you there!" he said. "What good do you get out of arguing? Especially on a day like this? Alexis, why don't you admit Old Markos is a great man? He is, you know."

"Then you think so too," said Penelope, much pleased. "We were looking for you. There's plenty of food."

"Certainly the old boy's a hero. But thank heaven I don't have to live with him," said the shepherd.

"I should hate both of you. I *do* hate both of you!" said Penelope, more for the sake of form than from actual anger. In truth, she too loved her grandfather more at a distance, as one might love a great cathedral, spectacular but hard to embrace. Still acting out her rage, she walked away from them, arms hugged together.

"Pen, I don't mean anything personal," said the shepherd. He had followed her and rested one hand upon her shoulder. "But I'd look rather ridiculous if your grandfather had me parading around with one of those great thundering blunderbusses."

"You look ridiculous anyway," she said, trying not to smile. She refused to look at him, but stared out at the horizon, where the land met the sea and the coast road was a tiny silver thread from which a long lazy haze of smoke stretched out and away.

"There seems to be a fire," she said.

"No," said the shepherd, "it's the army landing."

"The enemy!"

"Oh no, it's your allies," he told her. The smoke cloud was the dust rising from thousands of boots, tramping pair by pair, squad by squad, thousand upon thousand along the coast road as far as she could see.

"But why here? Why have they come here?"

"My dear, if you'd listen to the radio—yes, and to your grandfather—you'd know. Because Greece has fallen. They have no other place to go." These words, so gently spoken, came like a blow in the face.

Greece had fallen. Of course Penelope had heard that it was inevitable. Old Markos had been silent these last days, but she had heard the German voices on the Athens radio and she had known that the Greek army held only the beaches. But as long as they occupied the merest fragment of Greek soil, she had clung to an impossible hope:

they would rally like the legendary heroes. Now they were hopelessly defeated. They were here.

For a time the little group was silent, watching the dust. Then Penelope saw something in the near distance, a moving speck, and heard the insistent buzzing of a big blue fly: the motor of a lorry plowing up the dirt road to Aghios Miron. The shepherd remained with his flock but the others started hesitantly down the hill. Alexis took the lead. Penelope followed, her throat suddenly dry. She seemed to have a taste of pepper in her mouth as though she had bumped her nose.

They met the truck on the road. Three men were riding: a Greek driver, a British captain and his radio operator. Behind them trudged a company of soldiers. The driver stopped the car and spoke to them, asking in Greek the way to Aghios Miron. It came as a shock to Penelope that anyone should not know that.

Penelope and Alexis rode in the lorry. Penelope found her mood quickly changing: her first ride, beside an English captain, all of Aghios Miron to watch and admire! A moving crowd had formed about the lorry. Old Markos pushed the others aside. With him was the priest. Markos addressed the Greek driver who in turn translated into English a warm greeting. Markos pridefully outlined the steps he had taken to arm the village. The English captain smiled, listened, began to drum his fingers. Finally he leaned toward the driver. Again the driver translated, this time into Greek. "The Captain is delighted to hear all this," he said, "but his men are tired. He needs food for them, and shelter for a few days and if possible a guide to help examine the road's condition. A convoy of heavy trucks will be coming through."

"Heavy trucks! . . . Did you hear?"

"That means the gold!"

The whispers rustled through the crowd.

Without hesitation Old Markos offered the Metaxas farm as a headquarters. Turning to the priest he said, "The chapel will do for the men."

The little procession crawled into town with Penelope and Alexis still riding. The crowd pressed around the lorry, slowing it down. Penelope waved to her friends until Father Panagos, trotting alongside, asked if the boy in back were Alexis. She would have introduced them, had not Markos intervened, announcing as he had before that he had no grandson. The priest stared at his old companion, not understanding, and Penelope was too astonished to speak. Who was this old man? She was not sure any more.

With a piece of chalk the Captain scrawled on the front door of the Metaxas house *Captain R. Peachy, 21st New Zealand*. There were also a great many letters and numbers which no one understood, though Aghios Miron knew what was important, that this was Headquarters. The family was proud, particularly Old Markos, who hovered about, watching them assemble a radio set, dismantle a machine gun. The snap-snapping of steel parts sounded like the collision of dry bones.

The soldiers brought pride and excitement. They also brought increased dread of the impending war and for Penelope, the Captain ensconced in the corner of the family room with his equipment was as mysterious and isolated as a webbed spider, pulling this thread and that with no visible purpose. As she watched it seemed as though he were fate itself, testing a hundred lifelines.

Despite the soldiers, or because of them, there remained a gaiety in Aghios Miron which all could feel. The town was charged with a frantic spirit of carnival which began with the week-long wedding. The groom's family was sighted in the afternoon and the news spread. Their slow cavalcade appeared on the road. At the head rode the father, then the eldest sons: men of the grasslands, smelling of cheese. Penelope noticed that one bestrode his donkey with only one leg. Had he been a soldier? Was the war everywhere, even in a wedding party? The entire family followed, laden with gifts. With the addition of the wedding party, the revelry redoubled and mandolins creaked until dawn.

On Sunday the chapel bells rang at six. They would clang all day as they had done at Easter. Aghios Miron smelled of Easter again, of lamb, fish, cardamon seeds, entrails fried in oil. To Penelope it seemed that perhaps time had turned on its heel and taken a backward step, just one. If she concentrated, perhaps there would be another, then a third, always backward away from an uncertain future.

The wedding ceremony began at noon with a procession from the bride's house to the church. Father Panagos led. At his heels skipped a violinist, playing fast, then the bridal couple and their fathers attended by ten best men and the bridesmaids.

To Penelope the chapel seemed strangely altered, filled as it was with the stacked implements of war, but the priest read from the Bible as though he did not notice. When he came to the words, "to love and obey," the groom did what Cretan grooms had done for centuries: he stamped on his bride's toes. A murmur passed through the crowd. Those matrons who had seen the bride wince declared that he was a brute, while the men shook their heads and said sadly, "He's lost. He's too gentle, poor fellow."

Alexis must have been delighted by the custom. He

tried to find Penelope's foot with his own, but she was too quick for him. He received a sharp kick in the shins. "You're not very romantic," he protested, but Penelope raised a finger to her lips. "Hush, this is a serious wedding," she whispered. Afterward, she dared not look at Alexis, for fear of laughing.

Again the procession shuffled back to the bride's house, where gifts were presented, mostly silver coins and food. The groom's relatives brought cheese. They were bluff and hearty folk, round and solid as the cheese they manufactured. They embraced the bride, rubbing her cheeks affectionately until she had to go inside for rouge and powder.

Penelope and Alexis ate slivers of roast lamb and drank the wedding wine from tiny glasses. The wine was very old and its red hue had faded. They held their glasses by the outside rim, swinging them together so that the bottom edges shocked together, bounced away and struck with a series of impacts. Penelope called it "drinking like little frogs" because of the sound.

The wine sparkled golden in the glasses and presently the lamps were lit. These too were golden and blazed with a startling brilliance, lighting all the happy faces. Though Penelope did not sense it then, the lights were fading like the wine, along with all the things she had loved: her farm, the santuri at night, the glasses that clinked like little frogs.

The hired orchestra began to play and a group of men cleared a circle and stomped through "The Butcher's Dance." A Cretan bagpipe made a sound like that of angry bees and two others joined. Men and women formed a semicircle and danced, their arms stretched out. Alexis got up, and Penelope too. She tried a few steps, turned once, then twice around so quickly her skirts flowered about her legs. The group moved in perfect measure, gradually increasing in speed until they whirled over the trodden earth. "I'm a bird flying," thought Penelope, "a bird with gigantic wings and I shall never stop. The music and the dancing will never stop, never stop, this is the last dance, the last laughter, the last wine."

The dancing had to end. Already gypsies had edged into the cleared space. They danced for pay as well as for pleasure and they were skilled. A gaunt fellow with scrawny arms played a tambourine which seemed to come to life in his hands, leaping of its own accord into the air, finding his hands again. All the while its brass bells tinkled with metallic laughter: "this is the last, this is the last." A velvet-clad dancer joined him, snapping her fingers while the farmers stroked their mustaches, puffed out their chests, competing for her smiles. She danced in a slow stamping circle while coins thumped into the tambourine without a break in the rhythm. "Never let the dancing stop, for this is the last." No one talked and no one left. The rhythm and the revolving dancer held those who might otherwise have become aware of the hour and retired. More coins flew into the tambourine, coins thrifty farmers would regret in the morning. Let the coins never run out. Stop all the clocks, for this is the last. . . .

A goggle-eyed shepherd danced to one side, brandishing a rifle to show what a fierce fellow he was. He followed the gypsy's lead, cracked the gun against his knee and thunderously discharged a bullet through his calf. He fell screeching, but for an instant the dancing went on. The dancer brought her arms together, revolving like a red torch in the air. Do not stop. This is the last. But suddenly she stopped and let herself collapse, arms forward, palms up, in an attitude of prayer.

Two weeks later, Penelope was aroused in the dark by the sound of a machine. Outside the farmhouse it stopped and someone knocked. She opened the door to a British dispatch rider, who asked with hand signs and gestures for Captain Peachy. The soldiers conferred. A bugle rasped out and wakened the roosters. The village arose ahead of the sun. Lights moved in the gray dawn, engines started, coughed, stopped, started again. Captain Peachy conveyed through his driver that there had been an alert, and they had been called back to the airfield near Heraklion. "We'll hold them off if they come," said the Greek driver. "There's the gold. Forty-two tons of it! Can't let that fall into the wrong hands."

The motors had died away. The roosters grew silent in the spreading light. The calendar read Tuesday, the nineteenth of May, an ordinary day. Penelope told herself there was nothing changed. In the fields, in the village square nothing had changed. The radio had gone dead. She was glad of that, yet beneath the veneer of sameness there brewed a cold excitement she could not entirely deny. It was a matter of little things: Alexis scanning the sky as though he knew what to expect, the rumors that drew groups together, sent them scurrying away. Yet with the dusk, Aghios Miron went to bed, disappearing into the night as it had for hundreds of years.

The only thing wrong with the end of the day was Emmanuel. She had seen him oiling his hunting rifle. Why? He hadn't hunted in years. She could not sleep. The sheets were hot and rumpled and she lay half-conscious, half-asleep, while dreams poured over her, jostled her. Everything swayed, began to tremble. It was storming. The noise she had heard in her dreams merged gradually with the real world. She jerked into consciousness when the bed seemed to pass over a bump. With her eyes open she still heard the explosions of a storm. It rattled and growled from beyond the mountains to the west.

Shutters crashed, and outside there were voices. All over Aghios Miron people had heard the storm. They had flattened out on their beds and waited motionless, speechless with dread. It was thunder, please God, surely a storm to cure the drought.

Penelope sat on the edge of her bed. There was something wrong with the thunder. Not even a cloudburst sounded that way. Window glass shattered and the voices outside were louder. Her hand explored blindly for the table and the lamp, following the table until she touched the matches.

As she crossed the room to close the shutters she felt cold in her nightgown. At the window she saw no flashes of lightning, but there was a strange glow beyond the hills. From the casement she listened to the talk, learned that the storm was not a storm. She raised the lamp to her lips and gently blew it out.

part two

part two

eight

🙟🙟🙟🙟🙟🙟

AGHIOS MIRON: It will never be quite the same again since that morning when a horde of planes swept out of the northwest like a swarm of hungry locusts.

May 20, 1941. War was still a distant wonder to the village, a storm that was not a storm. But fifty miles away, at Suda Bay naval base and at the airfield at Meleme, 1280 Nazi aircraft were dropping bombs. Greek and British soldiers, lacking arms, weary from their defeat on the mainland, huddled in bunkers under the attack from the sky.

Old Markos mustered his recruits on the Metaxas farm. Old friends were there. Penelope saw Torgut Bey, the blacksmith, cradling in his arms a Turkish rifle of astounding length. There were men and boys she didn't know talking in whispers, bursting into high laughter. Patros, the baker of Aghios Miron, sat on a stool and tried to lace his boots but his stomach got in his way. He was mumbling to himself, "What am I doing here? I can't even load a gun. I'm a civilian. I'm more a civilian than most."

"No more stupid talk!" shouted Old Markos.

"Cheer up, old man," said Torgut Bey. "You'll go places with that spare tire around your middle!" He laughed briefly and then said, "We're all civilians, and today more than ever."

Everyone important was there and Penelope was proud of them all. Presently they would march away together, heroes, sweeping the enemy into the sea and that night there would undoubtedly be a great celebration in town with torches and fireworks. These things Penelope told herself, for as long as she had faith in her grandfather she would believe that those people who were brave and honest and in the right could never lose.

Emmanuel had stepped inside, and in a level voice which betrayed neither excitement nor fear said he was taking leave of his family. The men would go down to the airfield near Haraklion. They would take no risks, simply help out. There was no reason to worry. Emmanuel made it sound like a rather dull trip to market—but there was something wrong with his tone, with Penelope's entire world.

"Oh, Papa, don't!" She threw her arms around the big man. There was a pause like a sigh.

"I'll take care of myself," he said, "and with Markos and his friend on my side, what can happen? It's the enemy who isn't safe." He stiffened, trying to pull free, but Penelope's grip tightened at the moment it should have let go.

Outside, Father Panagos had arrived on a horse. Old Markos drew the butt of his rifle slowly along the ground, drawing circles. "All right, Emmanuel, what's going on?" And, after a pause, "Emmanuel, are you bringing that boy along? A little soldiering will do him good!" This time he put his lips to a crack in the front door and shouted. "I was just his age the first time! Emmanuel, let's go!"

Emmanuel kissed his daughter on the forehead, told her to look after Katerina. He put his hand on Alexis' shoulder. There was no mention of Alexis going with the Andarte. In the doorway Emmanuel said good-by to his wife as though there were no more barrier to their reunion than a day's plowing. Then he stepped through the door and the volunteers of Aghios Miron had surrounded him.

Father Panagos raised his staff and said, "Oh, Lord, we beg Your blessings on this company of Cretan men who now go to battle. Oh, Lord, forgive and protect us all." He unhitched a tiny white horse from an olive tree. Many hands helped him mount. Thirteen men in all left the farmhouse. Others waited to join them in the village.

With the little army out of sight, Katerina hurried to her room. She was not a woman accustomed to tears but, like a man, was ashamed of what she regarded as an extravagant waste of strength. Penelope stood alone in the doorway. The small troop had appeared again, a shuffling army of toy soldiers below the town, growing smaller. She could not distinguish which one was her father.

If this was war and war was glorious, why did she feel so ready to cry? Her grandfather's stories were coming true. The heroic days were here again, and yet she knew without admitting it to herself that something was monstrously wrong.

"Are you crying?" said Alexis, who had come in silently.

She looked at him fiercely. "No!"

"But I can see you are."

"You!" she said. "Why are you snooping around? You cowardly thing! What are you doing here? Go away! Just go away."

Alexis went. She had hurt him. She had driven something sharp into his pride, if he had any, and she did not care. She wanted to hurt, just as the world seemed to be hurting her. Her shoulders began to shake. With an indrawn breath she began to sob; she cried until she could hardly get her breath.

How long she had remained slumped in the doorway she did not know. Her grief and disillusionment had mellowed to self-pity when she became aware of a faint, far-off sound like the first droning flies of summer. Slowly the noise became deep and trembling. Penelope stood up and wiped her eyes. She saw Alexis running up the hill. Then suddenly, from behind the gray western ridge, war came with the shadows of terrible birds shrieking down the slopes. An endless airborne caravan thundered over Aghios Miron and descended upon the Heraklion airfield, which seemed at a distance to explode beneath them. Flowering like alien blossoms, paratroopers followed the bombs, dropping their white petals on Cretan soil.

In Aghios Miron, where no bombs fell and no paratroopers landed, the people vanished behind bolted doors. They waited for the keys to clang on the floors, the locks to burst on broken hinges, the walls to sag and fall upon them with crushing weight. Nothing happened. Gradually they emerged and found the visible world quite unaltered except for the explosions and pillars of oily smoke over the city.

For Penelope this occurrence, though remote, was as jarring as if she had been projected to the moon, where cratered soil was made to seem more harsh by the fierce glare of the sun. The old comfortable world of soft images, where war was a dignified contest among gentlemen, was gone. In ancient days, it was said, heroes occasionally fought among the Olympian gods. The little troops of peasants were not gods, or classical heroes shielded by gods, but men of everyday shape throwing themselves against a force more fearful than any array of Olympians. They had their human skill, their limited courage, their poor weapons and nothing more. When they died, they died. How could she have ever listened to that wild old man?

When she saw Alexis again she was ready to apologize. She needed sympathy. "I'm sorry for everything I said, Alexis," she told him. "You'll forgive me?"

Alexis did not answer at first. A horrible moment passed. At last he said, "Forget it; we're all upset."

"What can we do?" Penelope was ready to do anything to occupy her mind.

"You may as well rest. You'll need it later on."

But a great many thoughts were coursing in Penelope's brain. She needed to talk. "Even when I got you to tell about it, I never imagined it could be like that," she said, looking for assurance. Alexis could give her none. He freely admitted that he had never seen so many planes.

"Then they don't have a chance, do they? They'll never come back."

"I don't know," said Alexis. "I suppose somebody's got

to make a stand, only it's not going to be me. Not any more."

"If only Papa and the others hadn't gone. They'll be killed; when those bombers came I knew they'd be killed."

"You'd be surprised how few people get killed by bombs, when they know how to hide," said Alexis. "Believe me, I learned all about it, hiding on the road from Grevena. I wouldn't be here if I hadn't. Anyway, there are worse things than being killed."

"Having been killed so many times, I guess you know," said Penelope bitterly, wanting to attack something—anything—with her words.

"It's worse to be the one . . ." began Alexis. "Oh, come on. There are things we ought to do."

"No, tell me. What one?"

"The one that kills. That's the worst thing that can happen."

"You're an expert, is that right?"

"Before I came here," said Alexis, "I shot a man to death."

With a whistling of indrawn breath, Penelope clapped her hands over her mouth as though to retract the whole conversation. Alexis turned sharply away but did not leave. He stood with his back turned.

"When I did that," he said, "my whole life changed. When I was very young I thought how fine to be a soldier and kill the enemy. But then I did it, that's the thing. I did it. He wasn't much older than me and he was just standing there at the window."

"But Alexis, he might have killed you."

"He had a canteen in his hand. He only wanted a drink. We took him inside on my bed, Penny. He was on my bed and we brought him water but he couldn't swallow, and then he died."

"Alexis, I wish I knew what to say. Everything's so awful. I wish I could help you forget."

"I won't ever, as long as I live." Alexis spoke to one side as though addressing a ghost. "I can still see that face, like looking into a mirror. It almost seemed I shot myself, somehow."

Penelope could not answer or comfort him. Her brain was a confused and crowded place of horrors which a day before had not existed. "I'm going inside for a while," she told him.

She went through the door without looking back, walked directly to her own room, closed the door and fell face down on the great wooden bed, wishing the bed were the sea and she could drown in it, or become a mermaid. On second thought, she was too high-spirited to settle for drowning.

Thus one day passed, and another. The men of Aghios Miron did not return. There was no word, only a sad stumbling crowd of refugees which crowded the village and then dwindled away to the south, where it was rumored were ships that would take them away to the comparative safety of Egypt. No work was done in Aghios Miron. No one went into the fields. All waited for news and watched the sky where tiny silver insects flew, lazy dots circling Heraklion and dropping bombs. Penelope did not watch the planes. She kept to her room, to her bed, seeking refuge in its vast familiar softness.

On the second afternoon Alexis came into the room. He seemed almost gay. "You shouldn't lie around like this," he said. "There's lots to do."

"What? What can we do?" she said, looking at him with dull eyes, her face streaked with dried tears.

"Well, for one thing, you can wipe your face. Here . . ." He fished for a handkerchief. "It's not very clean, I'm afraid. . . ." But she took it. "Penny, don't use that dirty thing! . . . Well, I haven't blown my nose on it or anything. . . ."

"So, what is there to do?" she asked, returning the handkerchief.

"There's the farm to keep up," he said, "and there's something to see to, that you were talking about. Right here in the village there are a whole lot of trucks. They want food and help."

"What can I do for trucks?" she said irritably, flopping over again on the bed. "I'd just like to be able to sleep, but I can't."

"Penny," he said, "the trucks are full of gold. Right here in Aghios Miron there are forty-two tons of gold!"

nine

🙟🙟🙟🙟🙟🙟

In the deepest shadows under the awnings of Aghios Miron, under the Tree of Idleness where they could not be seen from the sky, crowded the trucks of gold. The idea was enough to rouse Penelope from her gloom, although the trucks themselves were drab and battered, and the soldiers who rode with them were no better; no flashing armor, no dignity in retreat, simply men parched with dust and weariness.

An officer who must have been in charge made an

appeal to the villagers. Water and food were needed or the gold would presently fall into enemy hands. Buckets and pots of water, bottles of old wine, all the liquid in thirsty Aghios Miron was brought out for the heroes. At last there was something useful she could do. Penelope carried down the great water jar from the corner. It was heavy, but she wanted to be tired—too tired to think, too tired to realize this was the last water beyond a green scum at the bottom of the well.

While the soldiers refreshed themselves, the peasants gathered, talking in small bunches. Listening, Penelope picked up snatches of information. The enemy held the airfield now. They were growing stronger every day. She asked for news of the men from Aghios Miron, but concerning them there were not even rumors.

Some children were trying to fit their fingers into the bullet holes spattered across the hood of one truck. They were laughing. Had they no memory, she wondered? Were they too young to be afraid? One of the boys poked his head under the lashed canvas. She would have liked to see the gold herself, but a guard shooed them away. The convoy commander spoke with the village elders about a truck which had broken down. Did Aghios Miron have an auto-maintenance shop? The elders had never heard of such a place. A blacksmith, then? Yes, but he had gone to war with Old Markos. In the end, two soldiers were dispatched to see what they could find around the village. One other thing the convoy needed: a guide to show them the way to Merka Bay on the south coast. From there an English destroyer was to carry off the gold before the island fell to the enemy. The elders conferred. They were farmers and shopkeepers and had never been farther than Heraklion. If Old Markos were here, he could guide them.

"Or the shepherd, El Greco," said Penelope. "But he might be anywhere in the hills."

"No, I saw him right here not fifteen minutes ago," said one of the elders. A frantic search might have begun for the little shepherd had he not emerged at this moment from the deep shade cast by the Tree of Idleness.

"At your disposal, Major," he said, and doffed his battered cap.

Had he been listening all along? Penelope had not seen him there, but apparently he had overheard every word and was prepared to go. How could he leave his sheep, she wondered. As though responding to this unvoiced question, he told the officer his sheep were independent creatures. They could look after themselves. Penelope expected the convoy to roll off immediately. She had forgotten the disabled truck. As long as the enemy was contained near the airfield they could delay, until the following night if need be.

With the deepening shadows Penelope returned home, again to worry and wonder about the missing men. The wildeyed refugees who had flown through town with reports of rout and terrible slaughter had filled her with conflicting doubts and nightmares. The soldiers had been calm. The way they puffed their cigarettes and said the front would hold had given her comfort. They were expecting reinforcements any day. But why, she asked herself, were they here, retreating with the gold, if all were going well?

Such were the doubts she went to bed with that night and wrestled with until dawn, the morning of the fourth day of war, when a boy came running down the road. Penelope was one of the first to see him; running, then walking a few steps, then running again. He ran straight for the square where a few old patriarchs had gathered around the broken truck to see how the work was coming.

The boy slumped down at a table, where the old men listened, got up and hurried off to report. Only the boy was left, too exhausted to move.

"What news?" asked Penelope.

"The men are coming back."

"All of them?"

"A few. Only a few."

Presently the first ones appeared, distant figures carrying a crude stretcher. For Penelope this was not an unusual sight. Often when a sheep broke its leg in the hills, a stretcher brought it home. But this load was heavier, longer than a sheep, too long for the litter. A heavy man was being carried that morning. A lane opened through the villagers and the stretcherbearers plodded through while Penelope pressed her hand hard against her temples and prayed that her father would be among those who walked.

Then, through half-closed eyes, she recognized the wounded man. It was Patros, the fat baker of Aghios Miron. He gazed up at the sky with a drowning face, as though he saw something he did not like.

"Old Patros did heroic things," said a man who had been there.

Penelope wanted to know about her father. She might have asked but her voice would not come. She simply waited to be told, while Patros groaned, "I'm dying." But the doctor who elbowed through the crowd said the baker had a bad smash, nothing more. Patros would be on crutches a while. His war was over.

"Oh, please! I'm dying, get a priest, get Papa Panagos!" pleaded the injured man, but he needed no priest, and received none—nor did any suffering citizen of Aghios Miron ever again receive comfort from Father Panagos, for he was not among those who returned.

While Penelope waited and watched with failing hope, the survivors came in by twos and threes, all weary, all discouraged, some injured, others being helped. There had been no place for them in the lines. They had fought for a while on their own, but they could not stop tanks with muzzle-loaders and horse pistols. "We're like an egg," said one. "Hurl it against a stone and the egg's smashed. Hurl the stone against the egg and it's the same thing." "Crete's finished and so are we," said another. Cut off by machine guns, they had opened fire with their old rifles. The machine guns crackled back and ten of the citizens became quiet bundles lying on the road. "You should have seen us with those machine guns," said one. "Tigers, just like tigers."

"You mean Old Markos was a tiger," said a man with a bandaged arm.

"Did they get him?" asked a woman, crossing herself. All of them dreaded the answer, for if Aghios Miron had a spirit and a will to survive it was that old man. Penelope closed her eyes. She knew her grandfather was dead.

"Old Markos?" said the man with the bandaged arm. "That old fury? He got them. He'll be along with Emmanuel. It's the old man's bad leg that slows them down."

Painfully, the Metaxas men returned from war. Markos lurched from side to side, his face very white and his lips pressed tightly together. Emmanuel kept his arm around his father until they neared the village. When Penelope and Katerina appeared in the doorway and ran toward them, Markos shook off his son and walked by himself.

Husband and wife embraced.

"Oh, Papa," Penelope cried. "Oh, Papa, I thought you'd been killed."

"Do I look that much like a ghost, Pen?" With this he burst out laughing. "Take a look. All you have to do is touch. That's skin there, real flesh, nothing leaking out."

Katerina turned to the old man. "Markos, are you all right?"

"Absolutely!" he said through clenched teeth.

"He'll not admit it," said Emmanuel, "but the old leg's giving out."

"Nonsense, I'm better than ever," said the old man, jaws clenched with pride and pain.

"Well, good leg or bad, we're finished," said Emmanuel. "It's only a matter of time. The army'll be falling back this way for a stand, and then into the mountains."

"Like the old days," said Markos.

"Now listen," said Emmanuel. "There isn't much time, so there can't be any arguments. There will be fighting here any day and after that those who remain will pay for the deeds of those who go on fighting. Wars are that way, and all of you are leaving tonight with the trucks."

This decision reached Penelope in the space of two heartbeats which seemed to strike one another. Immediately Markos protested. Katerina absolutely refused to go.

Old Markos never took orders. Occasionally he allowed the facts to persuade him. Emmanuel hesitated to confront him with them: that a man of eighty years might be a burden to mountain fighters. Instead, he appealed to the old man's vanity. "You've said yourself the shepherd's crazy. Would you trust all the gold in Greece to him? Would you put your grandchildren in the hands of a magician who can't tell the time of day? What do you say?"

At last the old man relented. He would lead the convoy, but he would be back once his family and the gold were safely off the island.

Emmanuel told him there was no use coming back. They could never hold the town by force. It was only a matter of delaying the advances.

"But what if we just stayed?" asked Penelope. "I mean, what if we go on farming like always and don't fight at all?"

"The enemy would come and take the house and make it their headquarters. They would take all the food and animals, and perhaps pay for it with their own money. Then if they left, the Andarte would come and make it their headquarters. They would take what was left and would not pay in any coin. No, we can't stay here, so listen to me," said Emmanuel. "This is the only thing to do. Far to the east, beyond the mountains of Lasithi, there is a town by the sea called Mirtos. If you do not escape on the English ship, go there. Find a Captain Sefakas. You know him, Father." Old Markos nodded. "When it is over here I will go there as well. With luck, he will take us to Alexandria, where I can join the army and be of some use in this war."

That was Emmanuel's plan and he glanced at the members of his family for any objections. Penelope said nothing. If she had opened her mouth, her voice would have burst out too loudly, and she would have cried when her arguments weren't of any use.

"Well then, it's settled," said Emmanuel.

It was far from settled. Husband, home, and family were the sources of Katerina's strength. She was not about to surrender them all at once. For Aghios Miron Katerina could fight as well as any man. In the end she had her way.

Penelope looked back and forth at the speakers, full of

disbelief. Every word seemed to twist a cord inside her, a cord which knotted and kinked and pulled tighter around her heart. She packed with numb fingers. War was a glory as old men remember it. But there was nothing glorious about being torn from home and family. Her entire life was here; this old bed, the windows that had mirrored her growing, the stone fence she had straddled in the sun. All were to be left.

"What will happen to the animals?" she asked her father. "Job, and the chickens, and the sheep?"

"You'll be taking Job," said Emmanuel, "and those old people who stay on in the village will care for the others."

"But you said it wouldn't be safe to stay."

"It won't," Emmanuel said, "but for the oldest ones it is safer than the road."

Late in the afternoon they were ready. The laden burro stood before the house. Parting was brief, filled with false optimism and restrained tears. "We'll see you soon." But when? When will we see you, and where? These were the unvoiced questions Penelope did not ask because she knew there were no answers.

Through the blazing light of afternoon, Old Markos led the burro. Penelope and Alexis followed, toward an olive grove outside the village where the trucks were waiting for darkness. The girl looked back once before the hills finally intervened. Aghios Miron lay in a glitter of beating light which made it appear detached, as though the houses and the hills had no contact with the earth.

Soldiers with leveled Sten guns stopped them. These were Greeks, some of them khaki-clad women. The lorries squatted in the deepest shade of the trees and Penelope could tell they were heavily laden by the deep tire scars they had left in the earth.

"Yasu!" shouted Markos in a voice that carried to the next valley. "Hey, I'm your guide here, let me pass!" Captain Stavro hurried up. From the way he looked them over, Penelope knew he did not like the idea of escorting refugees. He would have liked it even less if he had realized the bitterness between his two guides, Markos and El Greco.

"A guide, yes; we agreed to that," he said, "but what about these youngsters, and that mule there? We're a moving target, traveling at night, and fast."

In this moment Penelope seemed to see her future suspended from a scale with terrifying evenness. One side held home and loved ones, the other its weight of fear and danger and loneliness.

"I don't know," said Markos. "I'm not sure about the boy."

Penelope held her breath. The first measure seemed about to sink to safety.

"No," said Old Markos, "they may be young, but they can keep up. At least the girl can. They'll take their chances with the rest of us."

"As long as you understand there'll be no waiting for stragglers," said Captain Stavro. That was the end of hope. "And one other thing. I lack any authority over the English destroyer. Whether or not they take off refugees along with the gold is their business. Understand?" They nodded. "In that case, we've a map for you to see. Our other guide has already marked a route in red. I wonder if you agree with him." Old Markos glared at the map and the lines made by the shepherd.

"What do you think, old friend?" said El Greco. "Do I know this island?"

"If the roads aren't bombed yet," replied Markos grudgingly, "that way will do."

Penelope felt lost in these larger events. She had once lost a prized marble through a crack in the floor; she still dreamed of that round stone rolling away from her outstretched fingers. She was that marble now. . . .

With darkness, a motor coughed, then another. The two guides rode side by side in the first truck. They were in agreement about the road but the pace was tediously slow, for they went without lights. For Penelope and Alexis, who walked with Job, it was fast enough. With first light the convoy finally pulled aside under another grove of trees. They were exhausted and slumped down without even looking at the soles of their feet to see what the rough road had done to them.

A plague of sizzling flies settled everywhere—on leaves, on stones, on the travelers, who tossed and turned in restless sleep. Old Job bled a thick purple blood from their bites and Penelope, who could not sleep, slapped his shivering hide. "Job," she said, "you're too old for flies to treat you so badly. Would you feel better if they gave you bars of gold to carry?" The burro shook his jackrabbit ears.

At sundown, when the first coolness came into the air and it was possible really to sleep, the gold was moved again. They trudged beside the trucks, stumbling from exhaustion. Finally a young lieutenant, exceeding his authority, parted the canvas cover on one vehicle and shoved them inside. That night they slept on beds of gold while two old men in the lead truck tried to read a map by the glow of cigarettes.

The convoy arrived at a crossroad not shown on the map. The old men disagreed, argued, insulted one another until Markos, despite his thunderous voice, was overruled by Captain Stavro.

Penelope knew nothing of this. She lay in the jolting truck between sleep and wakefulness. When she was more awake, she wanted to laugh at just how uncomfortable gold could be, but her laughter sounded more like a sob. During the few hours she actually slept there was a constant dream of chasing a bright marble down corridors of darkness. She knew if she could ever catch and hold it she would be safe, but always the marble bounded away.

Before dawn they arrived at Merka Bay. The last miles were little more than a path. Wild pastures swept down from one ledge of rock to another into a deep gully where the trucks stopped, above the saber-slash of a bay where a destroyer would have to navigate in fifteen feet of muddy, turbulent water.

The sun rose over them, glared straight down, began to sink. The group of weary soldiers hardly moved, but re-freshed themselves with sleep and meager rations as they waited for the coming of the destroyer, HMS *Apache*. Somewhere below the horizon, she too waited for night. All waited, while the enemy planes webbed the sky, pass-ing overhead on their fatal errands. From the distant hills came the mutter of battle.

At dusk the soldiers began to stir again. Penelope gnawed a slice of bread, the kind called paximathi, which is so rough and hard it is said to resemble a miniature Crete. Paximathi is harsh against the teeth, and it occurred to her that for every tooth-bruising lump in the loaf there were a dozen actual mountain peaks in Crete. If they did not escape this night, how many of those peaks would they have to climb before it was ended? She put the bread aside and be-gan to secure her pack. She would have gone to her grandfather and asked him what he thought, but the old man sat apart, bolt upright, sulking because he knew his road was just as good as the shepherd's. Penelope could not know the reason for his mood, but she had guessed one thing about her grandfather. He would be glad to be rid of the gold and of his relatives, so that he might be free to fight in his own way.

Full darkness had arrived, and Penelope drowsed. There was not even the red and yellow glow of cigarettes to disturb the sleepers, and the black hours passed. It was almost dawn when a voice awakened her. "The ship has come!" Instantly there was activity and noise. Motors throbbed and the first truck jolted down the path. The sky was still dark but the scent of morning was in the air, the aroma of Mayflowers as heavy as at a wake.

Merka Bay, a jagged crack in Crete where the water foamed up white as milk glass, contained a dilapidated quay and, beside it, the solid black silhouette of a ship. The lorries groaned down the final grade over a stony lane to the jetty and crept slowly over the rotten wood. Every sound was magnified in that still hour before the dawn. It seemed to Penelope that all the mountains, all the trees had suspended their motion; there was no tremor in the beach grass, no lapping of waves. Even the fading stars stood still, listening.

A plane went over and vanished.

By now, the second truck was on the jetty. Soldiers and sailors tottered under tiny loads of gold. They seemed feeble, slow as in a dream, for gold is terribly heavy.

A blueness had come into the sky by the time the gold was loaded. The coins remained when a fighter plane swept so low that Penelope could clearly see the swastika on its tail. With jarring suddenness the destroyer fired and the spent shells splashed from the breeches bright as gold. Then the plane was gone and its was as though nothing had happened.

But dawn was coming. Daybreak strangled the night and Old Markos shook his fist skyward and cursed the sun.

"We'll have to get clear," said Alexis. He took Penelope by the arm.

"But why? What about the ship?"

"That was a scout plane," he said. "That's the way it goes; first a scout plane and then the bombers." He pulled her faster up the bank.

Yet the work continued. Boxes and leather sacks of coins were being loaded. If a bomb should strike them now the currency of all nations would sprinkle like confetti: British sovereigns, Turkish pounds, dinars, twenty-mark pieces. A bagful burst on the deck, rattling into the scuppers. No one stopped to sweep it up.

The second truckload of coins was on the quay when three bombers roared over the hill on a level with the treetops. "Down, get down!" hissed Alexis. She felt his hand on her back forcing her flat.

The first plane dove, leveled and released its bomb. Penelope could see the missile in flight, plummeting into the shallows where a black geyser rose like some sudden ocean tree above the decks. Water fell back. The second plane bore down into the cannon fire from the ship. As she remembered it, the plane was there one instant, sharp as death against the dawn sky, then vanished, leaving only a spreading gray smear in the air. The third bomber, jarred by the concussion, skittered through the sky like a skipped stone and buried itself in Merka Bay, its tail above the surface marking its fall.

All this happened in an instant. Alexis was on his feet, pulling her. "Now's our chance," he shouted, but the quay was empty of trucks as they ran. The old timber wharf sounded under their flying feet but the gangplank no longer hung from the ship's side. With metallic puppet voices, loudspeakers blared from the destroyer. "Hey, wait for us, you can't go without us!" shouted Alexis in Greek. An English sailor, not understanding, waved from the rail.

The *Apache* was pulling clear. Green water creamed around the sharp curving prow, carving up a solid trench which sent waves thundering along the narrow beaches. Penelope and Alexis watched it go, waving the gold out of sight, and Penelope felt a soaring of her spirits to see the ship safe. Though her opportunity for safety had been lost, she was in this moment a part of a victory.

The last hour of the night was over. The first hour of daylight had come.

"I don't think I'll be frightened of anything again," she told Alexis. "I hardly know what I was afraid of then."

"The same thing will frighten you the next time," Alexis said gently.

Plans remained to be made. The convoy of soldiers was returning to the front, which seemed to rage closer, more fiercely with the light. "I don't like leaving you here," said Captain Stavro, "but there is nothing I can do."

"We're not children any more," said Penelope.

"*Andartes,*" said Markos, and the single word, which signified guerrilla fighter, as he spoke it seemed to indicate a special creature, some mythological beast or a rare species of big game, dangerous and practically indestructible.

"God keep you in the hollow of his hand, Captain," said El Greco. Stavro saluted them.

"Go with the good," he said, and turned and went to the trucks, which presently rolled away leaving behind them one cropping burro and four Andartes.

"So," said Markos. "We are all together still." His tone was bitter. His fate was not his own, it seemed. "And the shepherd, he also chooses to stay, does he?"

"What would you suggest, old fellow?" said El Greco.

"That you do as I say, or go your own way. We are heading for the mountains," said Old Markos.

"If you intend, as I think you do, to end up in Mirtos, it would be easier to take the coast road," said the shepherd.

"The mountains!"

"But Grandfather, isn't El Greco right? Remember your leg," said Penelope.

The old warrior had made up his mind. No one was telling him what to do. They could take the coast road. He was bound for the mountains and without waiting to hear what they would say, he started off, leaning heavily on his rifle.

They watched him. Alexis was glad to see the old man depart. "If we stay with him we'll only get killed," he said.

Between those who stood and the one who limped away Penelope was torn. Once she would have followed her grandfather unhesitatingly to the highest, coldest peak in the world. Two days before, when the bombers had come over Aghios Miron and her dream of splendid war had vanished, she would not have followed him to paradise. Now she was divided between her friends and the old man who did not seem as self-sufficient as he once had. Alone in the mountains, what would become of him? On the verge of tears, she followed her grandfather.

ten

⚔⚔⚔⚔⚔⚔

Two figures plodded up the road to Lasithi, an old man fast burning out and a girl leading a burro. Many times throughout the day the girl had offered to help the old man, but always he had refused.

They passed stragglers, sitting beside the road, who still dreamed of the sea and the rescue boats that waited there. A few tried to tell the old man he was going the wrong way, but his wild eyes silenced them.

Occasionally Penelope stepped out of the dusty road

and breathed deeply. Her mouth was furry and dry from the dust and she allowed herself a few swallows of precious water from her bottle. There was very little water left, anywhere.

It was afternoon before she realized they were being followed. At first she had only known that two other figures were going against the refugee tide, away from the sea and escape. They were too far away to recognize. But as the scorching day wore on and the old man lagged they drew closer. By nightfall Penelope was certain and the knowledge was as satisfying as a cold jar of clear water.

Alexis and the shepherd did not catch up that night. At first Penelope was disappointed. Perhaps her eyes had tricked her. If it were really the shepherd and Alexis, why did they lag? Certainly they could not be as exhausted as the old man. With Alexis it might have been pride, but pride could never explain El Greco. Despite his comic show, his bantering, the shepherd was the wisest man she knew.

They had nothing to drink that night or in the morning. The island was drying up and her grandfather was almost finished. Though he denied it, Old Markos was sick. "All hawk and no spit, that's me. All hawk and no spit." Still he went on, raising one shoulder high and breathing loudly as a torn bellows.

Their pace had slowed. The others were catching up, enough for Penelope to notice round green objects in their arms. Melons! She should have realized before what the shepherd knew, that water in Crete had been sucked away into the hard round melons which grew in the fields beside the road. They might not be ripe, but she could almost hear them opening with a wet crackling sound.

"Look," she told the old man. "Look back. They're

...ging melons. They have water." He hunched his shoulders. He did not seem to hear. "*Grandfather!*"

"We can get along without their favors" was all he had to say. Stubborn as Achilles, the old man lurched forward again. He would not be overtaken or forced to endure compassion from those he held in contempt. With this realization, Penelope understood. She could almost see Alexis, eager to rejoin them immediately, regardless of a scene, and El Greco holding him back for the proper time when the old man and his pride were ready.

It was midday. The sun beat down on Penelope's head. The old man leaned on his gun. She had offered her arm again and been rejected. She had reminded him of the melons. The whole affair was such a foolish comedy, like the behavior of sulky little boys after a fist fight. It had to end, but she was not prepared when that end came abruptly, with the pounding of feet. Alexis and the shepherd were running, waving their arms wildly.

"Hide! Hide!" shouted the boy. "They're coming!"

Before the enemy appeared they managed to throw themselves down behind a low stone wall, too late to conceal the burro which grazed in plain sight. Penelope watched through a chink in the stone, saw dark gray turtles moving along the road smoothly and with impossible speed. The donkey stopped nibbling and watched as the turtles roared by in threes and fours. Seeing the mysterious turtle shapes and realizing they were the metal-clad heads of Nazi motorcyclists left her between fantasy and reality, like waking up in the middle of a nightmare. Whatever lurked beneath those steel shells she did not wish to encounter on the road or in her sleep. And yet, what if they were not armed and crouched behind a stone wall, what if they were farmers still, and Old Markos held a hoe instead of a gun?

Then would it matter what passed on the road? She did not know the answer.

Job, his rubbery lips drawn back, began to bray, but the motorcyclists never slowed. The last one passed and the sound died away. The four comrades lay beside the wall for a while. They were together again and more in need of companionship than ever now that they were within the enemy lines.

At last El Greco spoke. "I can show you a better place than this, unless you're too tired. What about the old fellow? He looks a wreck."

"No," growled Markos. "I am never tired . . . never!" He found his feet with the help of a rifle crutch. When El Greco asked him directly whether he could walk, Markos waved him on with the gun. The shepherd led them along a path made by goats through an olive grove where the sun filtered down more gently.

"Tongue-wagger," complained Old Markos.

"He's only trying to help," said Penelope.

"He's a miserable little man," said Markos to himself.

"He's a very sweet little man," said Penelope.

"Myself, I find him difficult." Markos cherished the last word and repeated it.

El Greco bounded ahead with Alexis beside him through fig and olive trees, a rippling green forest. It was eerie there, with cicadas throbbing in secret dens under the stiff green leaves. Now and then a gray leaf floated lazily down through shafts of light.

Penelope felt safe, and happy for the first time in many days—closed in, hidden away like a mouse in the corn. Not even sound penetrated. The war was blotted out.

She led Job over the hushed floor of fallen leaves, up and up through the tunnel of branches. The burro was snow-white from the dust, a ghost burro, bearing his pack limpingly but without complaint. Penelope stooped and examined the hoof, where a splinter had lodged. Gently she drew it out and Job nudged her with his head.

Before them the trees thinned and opened upon a stony platform, erected centuries before by a departed civilization. "Roman villa," said their guide, leaping up on a wall and hauling Alexis after him.

"It will do," admitted Old Markos. "How did you find it? Wandered here with your sheep, I suppose."

"What if I said I built it? Would that satisfy you?"

"But no one's going to believe that," said Alexis.

"Of course not," said the shepherd. "But, as the old man says, it will do."

The sun had already collapsed behind the White Mountains when they settled down for the night with only the shepherd's melons to refresh them. Though necessity united them as travelers, as campers they kept apart. Penelope and her grandfather settled under the trees. The others perched upon the villa floor for the night.

For the first time Penelope took care of her grandfather, found him moss for a pillow, tried to make his bad leg comfortable and thought of him as she never had before, as an old, old man. When he seemed to drop off she tried to sleep and could not, though for the first night in many there was no sound of war. She lay awake, wide-eyed, staring at the sky where an ocean of milk seemed to have foamed across the heavens. Old Markos twisted and threw his arms out wide. He mumbled in his sleep and she wondered whether he could keep going. Tomorrow, perhaps, but what about the days ahead? What about the mountains?

Cicadas shrilled in the dark.

Penelope stiffened, suddenly alert after a profound

sleep that had lasted an instant. Before she opened her eyes she knew something was standing beside her. At first she thought it was Job. Then she knew it was not.

The shepherd knelt over the old man's restless form. Penelope saw him plain as day and yet she knew he appeared in the heart of a dream. In one hand he held his pipe and with the other, smooth and cool as yellowed ivory, he touched Markos' forehead, softly, softly. "Old man," he seemed to say, "are all your hopes smashed? Breathe deeply, drink down the good cool Cretan air." He seemed to hold a leather bottle to the old man's lips. "Drink down the air from snowy Ida. I have it here, warm breezes stirring over Malia's lemon groves. Breathe, and remember, when you're too old for other dreams. Drink the air scented with olives, the good green wheat of Messara. We still have deeds to do, you and I. Breathe deeply and remember."

All this Penelope dreamed. She dreamed that El Greco cut the moon up into slices and offered them to her like the sections of a tangerine. When she actually awoke, or thought she did, it was still night. A small fire fallen to embers showed her the slumped-over shapes of Alexis and the shepherd, both sound asleep, and beside her Old Markos, slumbering for the first time like a child. Her grandfather lay with his head pillowed in his arms, mouth slightly agape. Penelope, in a moment of panic, bent close to make sure he was not dead. She felt the breath come and come again against her cheek, with all the sweet coolness of a hundred spring mornings, the freshness of deep pebbled wells, of whitewashed rooms.

Once again Penelope slept, in deep darkness below dreaming, until a hand on her shoulder roused her to bright morning sunlight. "Good morning," said Alexis. "I was worried about you, you slept so soundly. I was afraid you were sick."

"Where's Grandfather?" she asked.

"On ahead," said the boy. "Said he felt good and wanted to blaze the trail. He's one old fury, that's for certain, even if I can't stand him."

For a change, the air was brisk. The breeze from the mountains brought the cool air down with it, the smell of pine and orchards. They might have rested that day and traveled at night for safety but the lack of food and water drove them on, upward through perpetual olive groves. Among the trees there, white marble statues reared or lay full length: the forgotten figures of ancient Rome. One held a double flute to stony lips. It resembled a younger El Greco.

Their route was always upward toward the mountains, over roughening ground. They had overtaken Old Markos and once again the shepherd and Alexis led the way. Penelope accompanied her grandfather; his strides were longer, surer, than the day before. Behind them all came Job, his tiny hoofs ticking rapidly lest he be forgotten.

Where the olive groves thinned, foothills began. There were no olives here, or vines or gardens, but in the afternoon they discovered an abandoned settlement. "There's a spring nearby," said El Greco. As usual he was right. On the ledge overlooking the gorge Penelope found a thin trickle of water oozing from a hollow trunk. Job's head sank down between his knees. He drank and the others followed his example.

"You certainly know this country," said Penelope.

"Why, yes, I think I do," said the shepherd.

"Enough!" growled Old Markos. "Next you'll be saying you built this house, too."

El Greco said modestly, "Actually, there's a rather attractive little cemetery up the hill where some relatives are sleeping. That's how I know."

Penelope filled their water jars. Markos seized a gourdful and emptied it over his head, gasping and cursing at the coldness. He expelled his breath in a great gasp and did everything he could to appear vigorous.

"Listen to Grandfather blowing like a horse," said Penelope, encouraging the deception. "If I felt that good, I'd carry the rest of you on my back."

"Any time; I'm ready," said the old man. He would have done it, too, until his heart gave out.

While they climbed toward the cemetery something appeared in the sky. At first it could have been a hawk. Penelope might have ignored it had it not been for Alexis. "Run for cover!" he shouted. They began a lurching, lung-burning, toe-battering dash toward the cemetery as the speck turned into a black wide-winged wasp with dangling legs, and then a plane . . . diving.

Once again Alexis was thrusting Penelope ahead of him. "Behind the stones!" he shouted. This was a Turkish cemetery, a place of turbaned markers rearing at angles like marble people trying to draw themselves free of the earth. The little lizards stopped sunning themselves and darted into their holes while the plane came down with a hammering roar. Bright flame flickered along the wings.

Penelope threw herself face down. Alexis was beside her and the air above was a jarring confusion of red-and-black thunder. She couldn't breathe. She was deathly cold and opened her eyes but once, to see Alexis gnawing his lower lip. He smiled when he saw her and placed his hand over hers. There was a moment of silence as the plane whirled high. Penelope felt only the bumping of her heart, that faint pulse that had been with her always. She tried to imagine a time when that beating would suddenly stop. She could not. Then the howling engine again enveloped them, drowning the pulse; whine of metal against stone, the single small crack of a rifle as the plane passed over. The blood still beat in her forehead, throughout her entire body. That was how she first knew she was still alive.

When she looked again, she saw that the shepherd stood idly beside her, oblivious of what was going on in the sky. In a choked voice she told him to get down. He did not, but from his canteen poured water into a recess in a marble gravestone, saying, "There, now. I wonder what the birds have been doing with no one to fill their drinking wells."

"Please get down," she pleaded. "You'll be killed."

"Do you know," he said with the same maddening calm, "according to the Moslems, death is a caravan of rich spices and perfumes. They say death rides a jet-black camel and helps you up behind to ride across the deserts into paradise. What an idea!"

Penelope begged him to take cover, but he shook his head. "I don't expect to ride any black camel, not just yet." And, as Alexis was quick to point out, the plane had gone.

While El Greco systematically filled the little drinking cups on all the graves, the others found their feet and pinched themselves.

"You were right," Penelope told Alexis. "I was frightened, worse this time. I don't know if I could stand it again."

"I think you could," he assured her. "It gets to be a habit." To be comforted by Alexis seemed suddenly strange. Only weeks before he had fled from shadows. "If you'd been on the road from Grevena you wouldn't mind half so much, honestly. When you think about it, being shot at isn't so bad as long as you aren't hit. Think how that pilot must feel. If he's a human being at all he won't forget us or the others. We're the lucky ones, as long as none of us were hurt."

But Job had been hit—luckless to the end. The plane had cut him down. He seemed only to sleep and should have roused himself with Penelope's call, "Come on, Job, we've got to go," but there were blue and bloodless punctures along his woolly flank.

Alexis unfastened the burro's load. "Poor fellow," he said. "At least it was quick and painless." Though Job was as well loved as any burro could be, there was no time to mourn him. Their own lives had been brushed too close by death. They simply took what they could and left him, his blue beads still around his neck. Penelope wondered, wanting to cry, if death had come for him on a jet-black camel. Had Job ridden away with his legs all dangling down?

The heights of Lasithi loomed ahead, the cheerless, slippery gray surfaces glinting metallically. They climbed toward them through air increasingly thin and cold. The shepherd strolled ahead, untiring, never losing the trail. Alexis tried to keep pace. Barefoot he went from stone to stone, jerking his elbows as though the flapping might set his painful soles down more lightly. Penelope and her grandfather followed. Finally, without pretense, Old Markos leaned on the girl. Nothing had been said. She had merely offered her arm again and he had accepted it, though it must have been the most humiliating moment of his life.

They went silently, the old man brooding on his decrepitude, the girl wondering about a boy she could no longer understand. Penelope was afraid and angry. She wanted to hit back or cry with her head in Emmanuel's lap, but Alexis seemed calm, even happy. Could he find pleasure in this? She could have understood it if he had been cast in his grandfather's mold. Perhaps his earlier experiences on the Grevena road had steadied him or, perhaps—her next thought seemed scarcely credible—perhaps he wanted to be punished, even killed for the killing he had done. And El Greco was worse, standing up, a smiling target. If the world weren't totally mad, then Penelope had never been sane.

With the night came total darkness and they stopped for fear of falling until phantom day began with the rising moon. Then they went on, looking for shelter—a cave, some shepherd's hut, anything to shield them from the terrible cold. They found no resting place until a distant chapel showed itself, clean and white and glowing under the moon. The gate was ajar and they entered the haven, which seemed deserted, as though magically conceived by unseen hands. Bronze chandeliers shed a faint, unreal light upon the frescoed walls where angels, their hair bound back with gay ribbons, struck at demons sprung from cracks in the painted earth.

Old Markos dropped in a corner. His pack, which was still on his back, seemed to prop him up. One after another they let fall their loads and Penelope helped the old man off with his. "I've never been so tired," she thought. "I'll never be so tired again until the day I die." None of them had the strength to investigate the long corridors that led away from the chapel room. Had the enemy streamed down those passages on motorcycles, the little group would not have stirred itself, and indeed none of them did get up when a glow issued from one of the corridors and grew more brilliant.

eleven

꙰ ꙰ ꙰ ꙰ ꙰ ꙰

S uddenly a skull appeared
suspended in the gloomy
doorway. El Greco stood up, doffed his hat.

Sister Magdela was terribly tall and thin as doom. She
stood silently in the arch and peered into the chapel. In one
hand she held a branch of candles which cast a fragile globe
of light about her face.

Behind her followed Sister Sophia. Penelope was reminded of some pictures she had seen of Queen Victoria.
Plump and dumpy, Sister Sophia had a majesty about her

which did not show at first. It came from the soul. "Sister Magdela, what have we here?" she said in an imperious tone. She received no answer. Sister Magdela seldom spoke except to God, and her occasional words had nothing to do with practical matters.

"Well, someone speak up! What are you doing all over the floor? Where are you from?"

"A long way from here," said Penelope. "From Aghios Miron." Then the tale was told while the sisters listened; Sister Sophia with her eyes intent on the teller, Sister Magdela with her head inclined, whether by the weight of prayer or slumber it would have been hard to say.

"I see. Yes, I see," said Sister Sophia. "And you haven't seen your parents at all since then? . . . No, they haven't passed . . . and I suppose you're all starving. We haven't much, mind you, but we know how to share."

Sister Magdela led them to cells where they could spend the night. There, Sister Sophia talked of milk and cheese and the scarcity of food at the convent until Penelope's stomach ached and her conscience urged her to refuse refreshment. Never had hard beds seemed so soft. Never had rough fare tasted so sweet. Yet Markos lay on his bed, unable to eat, repeating that he was not hungry. Penelope managed to coax down a glass of milk, removed his battered boots and pulled the spread up to the old man's chin. She did it all very naturally, without even considering how odd it would have seemed just days before.

Penelope slept, to awake about six when a slanting ray of sunshine slid through a chink in the wall and struck her eyes. She rolled over and tried to go back to sleep but there was so much to think about, so much to decide. They were safe here, really safe for the first time. The security brought her parents vividly to mind. What of them? Once she had thought they could care for themselves no matter what. This she no longer believed. Any hope of finding them meant pressing on to Mirtos. How could any of them go on? Her thoughts revolved in circles, never finding answers. Then she heard singing and knew it was Sunday. Would the bells be clanging in Aghios Miron?

They stayed at the convent all that day. There was no talk of leaving. Old Markos never moved from bed. The others rediscovered their fatigue. Penelope and Alexis explored the convent with its sparse rooms, many of them empty. Smelling of sun-worn flowers, stony paths led away to stonier fields. There were only a few elderly women, black-clad, struggling with the unyielding soil. Such a community in the hills was accustomed to have men about to do the heavy work. The war had taken them, and many of the women as well, for not only women of God lived in such a place. Anyone disappointed in the world, seeking shelter, could come and stay, and work. Now, with the drought, and no one strong enough to make regular trips down the mountainside for supplies, the convent was dying.

In the afternoon Sister Sophia urged them to stay. She offered them shelter from the raging world in exchange for their young strength. They could save one another. El Greco refused to advise them. He was only a guide, he said. Alexis, who had lost his family long before, had small stake in reaching Mirtos. Though his mother might be in Alexandria, there were mountains, a sea to be crossed. He voted to stay.

Penelope was tormented by the thought of her parents waiting in Mirtos until Sister Sophia explained that the chapel had occasional visitors who could carry a message. There was plenty of space in the convent and a farmer's hands would be welcome.

"But my grandfather," said Penelope, "we could never persuade him."

"Moods can change," said the nun.

"Not his. I've known him a long time, and he has only one mood. He won't rest until he's back in his mountains with the Andarte."

"Yes, but you have heard about faith—and what it can move," said Sister Sophia. "Perhaps your grandfather will have a surprise for himself."

"I wouldn't like to tell him that," said Penelope.

"But you'd like to stay?"

"You don't know how much."

"Well, then," said the nun, "someone simply has to make a stand. Let me do it for you if you're afraid. . . . Yes, I think I can handle one old man." Suddenly, surprisingly, she laughed and her whole face was involved. "I might even enjoy the battle."

Infected with confidence, Penelope felt as though a stone had rolled away from her heart. They had found a refuge.

Several days passed during which she renewed herself. With Alexis, she began work in the fields while El Greco shored up the crumbling terraces to hold rainwater if it ever came. Everything seemed to be going well. Even Old Markos was recovering. He fed himself now, and she watched him prowling the room like a caged lion. She liked to see him getting better, all but the leg with its battle wounds. He could not be held much longer, and at last she told Sister Sophia that if he were ever to be persuaded to stay, the time had come.

Sister Sophia began gently at first, saying, "Soon you'll be well enough to do some light work, I think," as though no one could imagine his wanting to go.

"*Work?*"

"Yes, in the fields with the others. Surely you don't intend to live here on charity?"

That was right, thought Penelope. Markos always rose to a challenge. Nothing else could hold him.

"I intend to leave."

"You'll do no such thing. You're too old a man to jeopardize your health in those fearful mountains." Immediately Penelope realized this was a fatal mistake. The challenge had shifted ground.

"So I'm too old!" Were he not addressing a nun, Old Markos would have bellowed and pounded the table. Instead, he opened his mouth, displaying a flawless set of teeth. "I haven't lost my grip, not yet. I still have these to hang on with."

To Penelope, Sister Sophia seemed to puff herself out, to grow visibly in size. This was a nun who thrived on arguments, particularly when the obstinate stupidity of men was involved. She thrust her face very close to his and riveted his eyes with a terrible gaze. "I think we must be very clear about one thing," she said. "The mountains may be a place for a demented old man to scatter his bones but it is no place for this girl."

"God give me strength to endure," groaned Markos.

"Yes, and give me strength to endure you."

Their views were too far apart for communication. Markos had turned stiffly away, toward the mountains, and Sister Sophia had left him. As Penelope knew, this was only the first battle. Sister Sophia had won, for the old man made no effort to leave that day or the next. For the moment the hatchet was buried, its handle disturbingly near the surface.

Penelope began to feel at home. She worked the fields as though they were part of the Metaxas farm. She began to confide in Sister Sophia and from her learned what a prosperous place the convent had been. "If men could only use their strength against these rocks, not against each other." Hers was a simple faith: "I talk about God a great deal," she would say, "and I think His name must offend unholy people in times like these. Why else would they run away?" Then Penelope or Alexis would promise extravagantly to save the crop singlehanded. "There, there, I'm just playing for sympathy. Never mind me. I said that for effect. I'm no saint like Sister Magdela. She is one, you know. She lives the deeper life without thinking of harvests and food. That's why we practical ones have to keep that much busier."

"To feed the saints?" asked Penelope. Her question passed disregarded.

"There was a young woman here not long ago," said Sister Sophia, "an orphan. I raised her. She had ability. She wasn't a saint, mind you, or even a nun, but she could make this place run better than anyone. The others would follow her anywhere, for she had the gift of using people and getting the best out of each. I had hopes that Ariadne would take charge here. Then came the war. She left to join the Andarte and many of them went with her. They went to the mountains. They were just as misdirected as your grandfather, I think, and yet God has His purposes. Though we weep through the night, joy cometh in the morning. I tell myself that when I watch the soil blowing away—joy cometh in the morning." She put her arms around Penelope. "And now it almost seems as though the sun were coming up."

Finally there came the day Penelope had been dreading. Old Markos pronounced his readiness to depart. When Sister Sophia again confronted him, Markos tried at first to be conciliatory. Uncompromising by nature, the effort seemed actually physical.

Penelope held her breath. This argument would be the last.

"Then you won't reconsider? If not for your own sake . . ."

"I haven't come this far to be a farmer," said Old Markos. "What the others do is up to them, so let me be."

"*Andarte!*" said the nun. She pronounced the word with all the hatred she might have reserved for Satan. Penelope knew how she felt about these partisan fighters who from the old days had called themselves Andarte. Sister Sophia hated them for their stupidity. They might hurt the invader but never to the extent they hurt their own people. At the very least they left the fields to waste while for their deeds against the enemy, vengeance was executed upon the innocent: the old, the young, those who were peace-loving. "These Andarte are worse than tigers. At least the tiger does not understand what he does. You are willing to turn this boy and girl into wild beasts?"

Old Markos did not answer with words, but his stare was answer enough. Sister Sophia was equally adamant. If words had been lethal weapons, neither would have given up until one were dead.

"I see," said Sister Sophia, "that we had better have an honest discussion. Penny, if you don't mind, I think it would be best for you—for all of us. . . . Would you mind leaving?"

Penelope waited in the chapel. She prayed for them. It was some time before the nun reappeared. She looked exhausted and Penelope realized instantly that she had been crying. "I'm sorry," she said, "that we lost the argument."

"But we didn't," said Sister Sophia. "I believe we won."

"I can't believe it. What could you have possibly said?"

"That's between your grandfather and myself. It's for the best, and in time you'll understand," said the nun. "Then we'll have a talk."

Once again things returned to normal. There were no more arguments and Old Markos did not talk about the mountains. Except for the secret, Penelope would have felt at ease. She was suspicious. She kept her eye on Old Markos and inevitably the truth disclosed itself. From his testing of his legs on the near slopes, from an assortment of provisions in his bag, Penelope guessed. Old Markos was not a good liar when his granddaughter faced him down.

"You were going alone, without telling anyone."

"Well, what if I was?" said Markos, and turned abruptly, rudely away. "The rest of you are staying," he said, and then turned back for a moment. Sister Sophia had come into the doorway. Painful knowledge showed in the lines of her face. "Thank you, Sister," he said. "You've been more than kind. There is no reason for me to delay any longer." With this he went through the gate, his eyes boring into the ground.

The others watched him.

"He can't mean it," said Alexis.

"He'll go alone if he has to," said Penelope.

"Maybe it's better than all of us starving to death or falling from some cliff. Let him go, Pen."

"I can't, Alexis." It was a difficult decision and she feared she was giving the wrong answer. It was her heart speaking, certainly not her brain. "I don't know how to explain, but I can't."

They left well supplied; Sister Sophia ransacked the convent for them. She watched them go and Sister Magdela stood beside her, silent and deep in meditation. There was no one working in the fields. Under an eave of the chapel a few old women were spinning wool.

Penelope looked back and felt a hard bubble expand in her throat until it ached. It was hard to leave such sanctuary. If he had only gone before, without her knowing. Then her eyes swept upward, from valleys still bottomless in their shadows, to where her grandfather stood in the sun. He leaned heavily on his rifle, as Hercules must once have slumped on his staff when six labors lay behind, six before. His face was terribly pale and the stubble on his chin stood out like stiff gray prickles. He waited for them with the wind in his face, gazing down at his troubled island. The wind touched him with a colder breath than it had in other springs. From the old man, her gaze swept onward to the peaks, those sharp blades jutting out of Crete, jagged, steely, gnawed by rust.

They had provisions to last three hungry days, three days of cold and slow going, days in which Penelope saw no partisans, no animals, no signs of life.

"We've climbed enough mountains to get us to heaven and back, and where have we gotten to, anyway?" said Alexis.

This was the fourth day. Old Markos had mumbled something about the old days, when he had fought the Turks, and the mountains had been swarming with palakaris. But Penelope had told him to save his strength; she was tired of his fairy stories. After that, the old man was silent. Both Penelope and Alexis were needed to keep him going. He coughed rippingly and El Greco said with cheerful bad taste that he resembled an amateur's job of embalming.

"It's no use," said Penelope. "We'll never make it like this." No one argued. What she said was obviously true and needed only the admission. They helped the old man to a crevice behind some boulders which became a base for foraging in a countryside where goats could scarcely keep themselves alive.

Two days passed. They found a tiny spring for water but nothing to eat. Wild goats appeared occasionally, too far away to shoot. Nevertheless they tried to track them down.

On the third morning, they went scavenging, each in a different direction. El Greco said he would not shoot a goat even if he had the chance, so Penelope and Alexis carried the guns. With the pistol clenched in her fist, Penelope followed a grazing herd. If she came near enough would she pull the trigger? She would never be sure, for drawing closer to the animals she saw among them a donkey tethered under low boughs. Beside the donkey a copper cauldron of whey bubbled over a thorn fire. From branches dangled dripping bags of misithra, the liquid cheese of Crete. She saw no human beings, though a flabby hound dog appeared to beat the ground with a nervous tail. He did not bark while Penelope retreated to tell the others that the end of the world had been postponed.

With all three of them supporting the old man, they went down the slope. "There it is," she told them, pointing to the donkey, the cauldron and the dog, which shimmied anxiously toward them.

"Partisans, all right," said Alexis, "but where. . . ."

A precise voice, with the crispness of a gavel, cut him short.

"Halt! Who goes?"

The dog stopped moving and its tail drooped at an uncertain angle.

They heard a hammer click as it was drawn back. A gun barrel jutted from the shadows of a cave and the precise voice spoke again. "What do you want? Explain!"

"Friends," said Penelope.

"Step over where I can see you."

"Is the gun uncocked?" asked Penelope.

"My thumb is on the hammer," said the voice. "Come forward."

twelve

🙟🙟🙟🙟🙟

T he leader of partisans
stepped before them, gun
leveled. She was not tall or brawny, but her face was as
commanding as that of Medusa. The smile bore no more
warmth than a crack in a block of marble. It was the eyes
that held them all. Immediately Penelope sensed there was
something peculiar about those eyes.

She asked them where they were from; Penelope told
her. "Then you have been to the Convent of the Sisters of
Mercy?" She talked like a man, and Penelope tried to

answer her like one. Yes, they had seen the sisters. Yes, they were well, as well for the present as anyone could be who soon would have nothing to eat.

"That's enough," said the woman. Gun foremost, she herded them inside a cave. The place smelled of rancid butter, gun oil and bats. "Is this old man dying?" she said, prodding Markos with the barrel of her gun. The gesture was sharp, unfeeling, hard as the rocklike bones of her face. Yet Penelope sensed that this was not her true nature, only a callous façade to protect a doubting heart. Perhaps it was those beautiful, slightly swollen eyes and the way they softened into sadness when she heard of the hard-pressed nuns.

From a shadowy corner a man emerged, a spider of a man, always in motion. Penelope would remember him only for his mustache, like two little rolls of barbed wire under his nose. "This is Christo, my husband," said the woman. "You can call me Lady Messina. I'm in charge here. . . . We have a sick old grandfather here, Christo. He needs water."

"He doesn't look good," said Christo in a soft cobwebby voice. "No, indeed."

"I said the old man needs water," said Lady Messina. "Get him a drink before he rolls over and dies." Her tones were cool and modulated, yet the power of her personality shot out like sparks from a smoldering fire. Christo jumped to obey while she interrogated her ragged visitors. It was foolish enough for the Andarte to be up here fighting a war, she said, but for them to bring an old man, who could do no more than die . . . that was madness. Turning her face from one to another, she invited an explanation. Receiving none, she laid Markos out straight as a corpse. With what seemed sleight of hand, she suddenly ripped off his shirt and began tapping his chest with her fist. Markos coughed horribly but all resistance had abandoned him. He simply watched and waited, as a man who is about to be executed submits but gives no aid to the hangman.

With her ear to his chest Lady Messina paused, listening. "Either he's on his last legs or he's swallowed a cheap watch," she said.

Penelope said, "My grandfather'll be all right. You don't know him."

"No, I don't know him," said Lady Messina, who with her forefinger was forcing open the old man's mouth, "but I know something of disease. I'm not one of your medicine men who will talk about spirits and bitter airs living in an old man's chest. And I know this, if he does not have pneumonia now, he will before these mountains are through with him."

"You leave him alone," said Penelope. "I've been taking care of him."

"And not very well," said Lady Messina. "Listen to me. He wants medication or he will die."

Finally they cooperated. To the old man's lips Penelope held a potion of vinegar and ouzo while Lady Messina applied a hot cloth to his bad leg. "He's full of bullet holes, your grandfather," she said. Her tone was very low and it seemed to Penelope there was a note of admiration in her voice. "Perhaps he will outlive death after all."

With the dusk, the other partisans arrived, dark and dangerous men like chunks of rock torn free from one great boulder. They glared at the new arrivals, grunted and sat down without another word except from the last and largest. "Penelope!" he bellowed. She sprang up with a cry of joy on seeing the blacksmith, Torgut Bey.

"Damn my missing ear, but it's a small world," he

146

boomed. "Is that the old boy himself I see sleeping there?"

"He's not . . ." Penelope was going to say "conscious" but changed it to "awake. Please, he needs sleep."

The Turk examined the inert form with a wistful air. "I'd almost forgotten what an ugly old goat he is. He'll be all right, won't he?"

"So this is the Markos. Markos, the grand old warrior," said Lady Messina. "At least, what's left of him." They all knew his reputation and regarded his decline as an ill omen. With the drought, with heroes like Old Markos failing, how long could they keep up the fight?

Finally Torgut Bey introduced the others, men from all over Crete, all fighters. Few words were exchanged. The smell of food was in the air and they were interested only in that. Lady Messina fed them all, did the talking when a decision was needed, led them when there was danger and nursed them back to health when they were ill, and at times sat alone, brooding, with the most gloomy face Penelope had ever seen. In time she would admire this woman as they did, with the same wondering respect she would have had for Penthesilea, the Amazon queen.

Now Lady Messina prepared the meal over a brushwood fire inside the cave. Eyes watered from the smoke, for a blanket hung across the cave's entrance to prevent its escape. The enemy had secured the lowlands and there were reports of patrols and paratroopers in the hills. For the Andartes, long life would be measured in terms of such precautions.

Lady Messina stirred a simmering kettle of lambs'-head stew. She portioned it out, and Alexis took two bowls to Penelope.

"How's it going?" he asked. "Do you think he can swallow?"

"He has to," said Penelope, raising a spoon to her grandfather's lips. The cords of his throat worked slowly, but he ate a great deal for a sick man.

"You'd make an awfully fine nurse, Penny," said Alexis. "I used to think you were sort of—well—irresponsible, but you're doing wonderfully."

"What else can I do?" she asked, having as much trouble receiving the compliment as Alexis had delivering it.

"If you weren't here," he said "I could never help him. He wouldn't eat for me."

"Of course he would," said Penelope. "What you don't have is any respect for yourself. Why, I bet if you had to, you could fight. I mean if you wanted to. But I'm glad you're not a fighter, Alexis."

"Well, I know I won't ever be that, but being a doctor . . . that's something. I'd like to give back life, not take it away. After what happened, I feel I owe one life at least."

"Better get yourself some supper," she told him, trying to cut short the unhappiness which had crept into Alexis' voice.

Penelope did not eat until her grandfather's bowl was empty. Then she closed her mind to everything but the good taste in her mouth and the warmth going down, spreading through her body. She drained her portion until nothing remained but a vacantly staring sheep's eyeball. This she regarded as good luck, and with slow deliberation she popped it into her mouth.

At length a conversation started. Penelope sat back in the shadows beside her sleeping grandfather. She took no part. The partisans were out of touch with the larger war and they listened attentively as Alexis told how the government gold was saved.

"Then you aren't here to fight?" said Christo. This was curiosity, not accusation. "Thought you were a queer outfit. What a way to get to the sea."

Alexis explained that Old Markos had made the decision.

"We cannot look to the old men forever," said Lady Messina. "Times change. It is the young men, this boy, who will build the Crete of tomorrow."

Alexis said he was not Cretan.

"But you look like a fellow who could hold a gun and fire it," said one of the partisans.

"Right between the eyes," said another, grinning at Alexis with one eye squinting down an imaginary sight. Almost reluctantly Penelope had begun to listen. She was remembering a time when Alexis had hidden under a table.

When Alexis declared that he would never take part in war, the Andarte said, "Suppose people were shooting at you?"

"I don't care. I'd rather die than shoot back."

"Good boy," said El Greco, and silently Penelope thanked the shepherd. But the Andarte were not pleased. This was a boy they could not understand.

"A man must be ready to die for his country," said one of the younger men. "When I was your age, I would have given my right arm for a rifle."

"So now, Alexis, you have heard the opinion of Chardos," said Lady Messina. The others were reverently silent, as though all along they had been waiting for her to tell them what to think. "But Chardos is not a very thoughtful person, Alexis," she said. "Picture him with a rifle and one arm to use it." Her smile was one in which the eyes took no part. "I don't know; sometimes I think there are sensible reasons for being here. But we're not all in love with glory like Chardos. It is often better to live for one's country than to die for it. One can become a monk or a nun. I almost tried that once. We're not all fools like Chardos."

Penelope expected Alexis to bolt at any moment. She wanted to help but didn't know how.

"Who knows," said Lady Messina. "The important questions never have answers, not answers you can catch hold of. That's why I'm not in a convent now. Perhaps Chardos is right. He may go to the Elysian Fields after all. When soldiers are killed they never come back to tell us it was all a mistake. And if they live, they may have a kind of fame. They'll have stories and perhaps a scar to show their grandchildren, like that sick old man. When they're old, nothing will be left but the stories, which will be glorious and not like war at all."

Penelope knew the woman was right. For years she had listened to the old stories and believed in the beauty and glory of war. It had taken only a few days to destroy ten years of storytelling. But if the stories were only lies, why were they all here? Why were they fighting?

"Many have gone away in boats," said Alexis.

"That is true," said the woman, "but some of us love Crete so much, to leave would be a kind of dying. We must keep this island any way we can, for if we fail we may as well be dead."

As Penelope looked at her, the bones in that thin face seemed to press more tightly against the flesh and the eyes were far too old for such a young woman.

"Whatever you say, I haven't much use for a boy who won't defend his country. What's the matter with you, Alexis?" said Chardos.

"Leave him alone," said Lady Messina. "God knows, if there were more like him, we'd be better off."

"But there never will be, that's the thing. There never will be and you know it. That's why you're here," said Chardos, who rose with these words and disappeared outside.

"Don't let that hothead bother you," said Lady Messina. "You're welcome, Alexis, and the rest of you, whether you intend to fight or not——" Here she hesitated. It seemed to Penelope that for the first time the leader of the Andarte was at a loss for words, or rather that two sets of words struggled for the upper hand, one set very sure and patriotic, the other sadly idealistic. Finally she said, "When I was younger, I used to believe as you, that killing was wrong, no matter what the reason. You see, I was raised by nuns who want the world to be perfect like themselves. Perhaps I'm a pessimist, but I don't think this sick world is going to be cured by good example. When I tried being an angel like the sisters, I became afraid of mirrors. I was afraid of seeing a fool."

Like a period, she had set this cheerless jest at the end of the discussion. But Penelope knew that for Lady Messina the debate went on and on, leaving a festering wound under the stiff and unyielding exterior. From her eyes the pain shone forth, eyes that were so sorrowful and lonely that Penelope, staring into them, began to suffer too.

"The truth is, we need men," said Lady Messina. Abruptly her mood had been put aside. "What do you say?" She looked first at El Greco, then at Alexis.

"No, I'm sorry," said the boy. "There are people we must find in Mirtos."

"And from Mirtos, where?"

"I don't know," said Alexis, but Penelope interjected "To Alexandria, we'll go to Alexandria by ship."

"This war is not to be run away from," said Lady Messina. "It will get to Alexandria before you. Besides, there are no more ships."

"But there's a Captain Sefakas in Mirtos," said Penelope.

"Ah, Sefakas, the one who paints green roses and red bluebirds on his boat. Perhaps there is no blood in his veins, that one, only blue sea water. Sefakas might be one to risk his boat, but I have heard there are a great many trying to leave the island through Mirtos, too many for the fishing boats. Besides, what will your grandfather say when he comes around? He belongs with us, I think, in the mountains."

"He will die of the mountains," said Penelope. El Greco said nothing. He had known the old warrior longer than Penelope had.

"Nevertheless, you'll be with us a while, until he recovers," said Lady Messina, and with this the conversation ended.

The days that followed were filled with rest and good food. Each day began in cave darkness with the crash of metal: Lady Messina applying a rifle butt to a copper pot. Routine, she said, is at the heart of military discipline.

With Penelope's constant care, Old Markos recovered gradually. He had shed none of his fervor and talked endlessly with Torgut Bey of the old days, though the Turk scarcely shared his nostalgia. He had left an ear behind him.

While Old Markos dreamed, his three companions made plans. They watched him improve in health until the day Penelope told her grandfather they were leaving.

An explosion followed.

"So I'm still too old for the mountains, going to be put out to pasture! I'll be hanged if I'll leave! I put up with a whole lot of nonsense because I thought I was dying. You, you thought I was dying and took over, you and that boy. Well, that's all over now. There's nothing wrong with me that some good fighting won't cure." The old man stamped around the cave and was no more tractable than a bear with rabies.

"Stay, then, and the rest of us will go," said Penelope.

"You won't get anywhere without a guide," said Old Markos.

"But we have El Greco."

"That worthless shepherd!"

"Your grandfather's right," said Lady Messina. "You'd never make it."

"We made it this far," said Penelope, "because of Grandfather. We didn't want to come. We could have stayed at the convent and been safe. We might have been of help."

"What do you mean, help?" said Lady Messina.

"To those poor nuns, but you know what I'm talking about."

"Do I?" said Lady Messina, a stern tigress. She did not even pretend to smile. "What do you mean?"

With obstinate desperation Penelope disclosed her thoughts. "If it hadn't been for a person called Ariadne, they wouldn't be about to starve. That's your name isn't it—Ariadne?"

"And if it were, what then?" said Lady Messina. Her tone, as though a thorn had been suddenly driven under her fingernail, was a complete admission.

"You're the one they were counting on," said Penelope. "You and these Andarte, to keep the convent going, but you had to fight and so everyone left them."

There was a long hesitation while Lady Messina took a deep breath and slowly let it out. Finally she said, "You make it sound very cruel. Perhaps I am cruel. Is that how I seem to you?"

It was difficult for Penelope to answer at all, for she had come to respect Lady Messina. "I don't know that," she said. "I only know you were wrong."

"Often I agree with you," said Lady Messina, "even when I am asleep. Did Sister Sophia tell you this, that she had raised me as an orphan? That until the day I left with her farmers I called her Mother?" Such warring emotions might have destroyed an ordinary heart, but Lady Messina ruled her conduct with unyielding determination. "Let me confess one thing, and then we will forget all this. I may seem to know exactly what I'm doing and exactly what is right. I don't, but there are people here who depend on me. They believe, and that is enough. I cannot let them down and when I have doubts I banish them ruthlessly. I must act twice as strong. Can you understand that?"

Penelope could not understand, unless Lady Messina hated herself. She had no answer. She looked at the ground.

"You are entitled to your opinions," said Lady Messina. "You are probably right, but there is one thing, a practical matter, about which I am not wrong. There are paratroopers between here and Mirtos. You could not get through."

Penelope said, "Then it's just as well we're not taking Grandfather. His leg would only make it more difficult."

"What? My leg! There is absolutely nothing wrong

with this leg. There isn't one of you I won't walk into the ground!"

"But the paratroopers. . . ."

"The paratroopers be hanged!" he bellowed, and would have throttled any one of them who said he was not leading the way to Mirtos.

A day one week away was chosen. The intervening time went quickly while Markos practiced walking and the partisans came and went on their deadly missions. The eve of departure arrived with a cold, clear night in the mountains.

El Greco looked up at the sky, which glittered with stars. "One for every year," he said, and then exclaimed, "Look, look there, a shooting star! You can almost hear it sizzle. An Arab would tell you that shooting stars are rocks the heavenly host throws to frighten off evil djinns who try to creep into paradise."

"And if the stones miss, will they fall on Crete?" said Penelope.

"Yes, all the way down to this old dragon, to wake it up."

"Why do you always call Crete a dragon?"

"That's what she is to me, Pen," said the shepherd, "a dragon sleeping in the sea. It's the way she looks, long and narrow and rugged. It's the way she used to act, years ago . . . but you ought to be getting some sleep."

"I can't," said Penelope. "I'm frightened of tomorrow. I wouldn't want to say so to Alexis, but I am."

"It would be convenient if we could fly away from days like tomorrow. Remember the wings we talked about?"

"And I wanted a pair but you said they weren't made any more."

"What if I was wrong then, and I had another pair right here?"

"That would be wonderful."

"Would you strap them on and fly away from all this?"

"Yes, above the bombers."

"What about your grandfather?" said El Greco. "And your parents, waiting in Mirtos? But it isn't really up to you to worry, is it? You could fly to the stars on a night like this. They are so very bright and close you can almost touch them." El Greco reached up and closed his fist. "There, I have one."

"Open your hand; let me see."

"Oh, no, it will blind you."

"Open your hand."

He opened his hand. Nothing. "Too late," he said. "That one's burned out . . . but with wings, you can catch your own."

"You know I couldn't use them even if they were real," she said. "If I only knew what would become of us when we get to Mirtos."

"Well, if you get there, and you're lucky, perhaps you'll find a boat and go to Alexandria. Your father was talking about joining the Imperial Army, what's left of it. I don't think he believes in this partisan fighting."

"Would Markos be too old to join the army?"

"Far too old," said the shepherd. "But not even your father can move him from his island. If he's got one good fight left, he'll have it here."

"And what if none of us gets away?" said Penelope. "I'm not so worried about me, but Alexis." The words came thoughtlessly. They surprised her and yet they were true. Not long ago she would have worried first about her own safety.

"I wouldn't worry about him," said El Greco. "He's a boy who's growing up fast."

"Too fast?"

"In days like these we all grow old too fast," said the shepherd. "When I look at you, Pen . . . why, you used to sit on my knee, and I'd tell you tales. Remember? Remember Pegasus with his tail streaming in the wind? And the one about the mermaid who rose up from the sea on stormy nights to ask sea captains whether Alexander the Great still lived?"

"And he'd have to answer 'Yes, my lady, he reigns and keeps the world at peace,' or else she'd sink the ship. Of course I remember."

"But they seem a long time ago, and not very important, don't they?" said the shepherd. "You didn't have a cousin to worry about then, or a grandfather to care for."

Penelope would have liked to say that the stories were still important. She would never forget them, but they had existence only in the smaller world of her childhood, a world which seemed suddenly very far away.

El Greco said, "That's why I say we're all growing older. If you had any idea how ancient I feel tonight. Centuries. No, older, old as the stars."

"But how old are you, honestly?"

"Old enough to need a long, long sleep. So, good night, Penelope, and don't worry. Things will turn out. You'll see. I'll take care of everything."

On the last night Penelope slept on the hard floor of the cave as soundly as she had once slept in her own bed. With El Greco there, she was as confident as she would have been with an angel guarding each corner of her blanket. The last night ended when the sun slid inside, discovered the rifle barrels and moved on, exploring the sleepers.

Alexis stood up with a great yawn. Slowly, the others crawled out of their blankets. Lady Messina cautioned them at the entrance, but Old Markos brushed her aside. "What do you think, woman," he said scornfully, "that we'll go down like a wedding procession singing hosannahs? Are we carrying banners or blowing horns? Look after your own neck, young woman."

He turned and again strode away, refusing Penelope's hand, refusing to lean on his rifle though the effort must have been excruciating.

Penelope did not depart easily. This dark and fetid cavern, too, had become a home. She took her leave of Lady Messina. If there had been any way of apologizing she would have, but what she had said she still believed.

"We will take food to the convent," said Lady Messina. "I will arrange everything. You need not feel sorry for them."

"I won't," said Penelope. "I feel sorry for you." There was nothing patronizing in her tone.

With this she followed her grandfather, as she always had, as she always would, like it or not.

They trudged all that day through the mountains, going always southeast toward the sea which never showed itself. Penelope walked with Alexis, whose thoughts were solely on Alexandria. "After all," he said, "we've almost got the same name." He would admit no obstacles, not even the difficulty of persuading a fisherman to risk his caïque and his life on a dangerous, profitless voyage to Egypt. Soon both families would be safe, he said. "The one thing that puzzles me is what El Greco intends to do. He keeps coming along and I guess we need him, but has he said anything about his own plans afterward?"

Penelope said, "Sometimes he talks about going home."

"Aghios Miron?"

"No, some other island far from Crete where his people come from. Do you suppose he'll get there one day?"

"El Greco's an old man. . . . He'll get there."

"You mean he'll find a boat too?"

"No, not like that. He's older than he seems. He'll die."

"There must be another way to get back," said Penelope.

Alexis said, "Right now, I don't know any other."

thirteen

᭠᭠᭠᭠᭠

L̶ate that afternoon El
Greco found a cave, so
well concealed he must have been there before to find it
at all. There they threw down their packs and would have
slumped down too, but for the knowledge that the night
would bring the white-wolf cold of the mountains. No fuel
could be found in the cave itself, so Penelope and Alexis
emerged into the glaring sunlight of early evening. Far
to the west the sun slid like a wheel of burning gold over
the last hills. They were tired and had little daylight left.

The valley shadows had already passed them when Penelope started. She seemed to hear a cry far off. For a moment she thought it was only the sound of the wind in the darkness. The sound came again, more insistent, the thin voice of an animal in pain.

"What was that noise?" she said.

"I only hear the wind blowing over the stones."

"No, I mean that noise now. What is the wind doing?"

"Nothing," said Alexis. "You're imagining."

Perhaps it was only the wind. She felt the cold of it burrowing into her clothes. There was no time to waste.

They were groping through the last dusk for wood when Penelope, glancing up, noticed what seemed to a gigantic flower blooming on an upper slope. A gust stirred it and a silhouetted figure rose, leaned toward her. It settled to rise again, unsteadily: tall, indistinct as a vapor escaping from the earth.

Suddenly she was more afraid than she had ever been. This thing, this nightmare monster seemed sprung from the heart of some forgotten dream. Had it seen her? She did not scream but held her panic behind her teeth and grabbed Alexis' arm. The figure had vanished, but the flowering shape remained, rustling with the breeze.

"It's one of them!" hissed Alexis.

"No!"

"I'll see." Alexis went closer, Penelope hesitantly following. Could this crumpled shape be one that had bombed from a thousand planes, one that had moved along the road like a fleet turtle? This wretched creature could not be that terror that had invaded her life.

"He's a paratrooper," said Alexis calmly. "That flower of yours is his chute. Now his leg's broken."

"No, I saw him stand. That's what frightened me."

"The chute must have pulled him up," said Alexis. "He's helpless."

"We ought to run and tell."

The wounded man pleaded with gestures, whimpered like a run-over dog. He could not move, and he had no weapon.

"If you tell, Markos will kill him."

"No, he'd be our prisoner."

"You know Grandfather better than that. If you want to kill him, here's a stone. Go ahead, use it. He's worse than Judas. He's why the world's going to pieces. Here's a stone." She would not touch the chunk of rock, a weapon she could have hurled with all the fear and anger of these last desperate days.

She knew that Alexis had reached a crisis of some sort. He was appealing to her as though to someone older and stronger than himself and it made her weak. She was too tired and frightened.

"Please, Penny. If we pretend to forget, what can he do to us? We could give him water and a little food, even bandage his leg and find him a stick. He might make it. . . . Penny?" She did not answer, but stared at the tormented face of the enemy in the darkness. Face to face she hated no one, wished no one pain. If somehow it would put an end to suffering, she would give up her island, her parents, live alone in a desert; anything to end this war. If the world were out of joint, let others force it back . . . she was too tired. It made her head feel huge and drafty even to think of it. Yet there was no escape. She could not be a nun in the midst of suffering. Alexis' desperation was simply something new to be borne.

"Penelope, I told you how I killed one of them, but you don't know how it was. Just a fellow like that standing in the window of the house were I lived. I shot him four times. He didn't say a thing. He just tried to put his hands to his chest and then he fell. He landed on one of our chickens and crushed it flat with his body. But worst of all, he had no gun, just an empty canteen beside him, Penny, and I shot him. I shot him because he had one of those helmets on his head, and all he wanted was water. Penny, don't you see, if we help now, and don't tell anyone, it would almost make up for what I did."

She could see his face clearly in the first moonlight. His features looked drawn and haggard. The decision was hers to make.

"I'll do anything you want, Alexis."

Penelope found herself excited by her own boldness of resolution. She no longer had to think. They gave the man water and cut him free of the parachute lines. Alexis offered him bread and cheese which he could not swallow, fashioned a crutch from a long stick and helped him down to the mountain road a quarter of a mile below. At the curve of the road they left him, with a jar of water and some food. They could do no more, but they had given an enemy soldier all the luck he would ever have. They had saved him from death at the hands of nature. Now it was a question of whether the Andarte or his own patrols found him first.

"You're not angry, Penny, are you? You're not mad we did that?" asked Alexis.

"I'm just tired," said Penelope, "and I hope in the morning we don't pass that way, and maybe you'll stop feeling so guilty about what you did."

"I feel better now," said Alexis, "and Penny. . . . I think you're really fine."

"Just because I don't want to be a murderer?"

"You know I don't mean that. I mean the way you listen to people and always help out, as though this wasn't as hard for you as for the rest of us. I know how you feel about leaving home, but it won't be all bad in Alexandria. We'll see new things and you'll learn more than you'd ever learn here. We'll get jobs at a hospital."

Before they located the cave again the moon was high overhead, a full moon with a scarf of cloud stretched across it like a bandit's mask.

They cooked their evening meal over a meager fire of brushwood and brambles that Penelope and Alexis had gathered from the slopes. If the two talked secretly, if their eyes were wide with excitement, the others did not notice. Old Markos sprawled in the faint warmth like a burned-out log while Penelope and Alexis whispered, imagining wonderful things to come. Throughout the night in the drafty cave they pushed the future on and on until the war was over and they returned home famous, wealthy and worldly. And the best of it all for Penelope was Alexis. Despite the pallor of his face, she saw in him a new repose.

Next morning with the first dull dawn they followed a river that runs from the mountains of Lasithi down through the hills. It is a river with clear cold water in the spring when the snow is melting from above, but when the snow is gone the river dries up. In the early summer the hills are red and bare. The dry river bed cuts through the soil like an open wound. If rain should come, the earth would bleed from the wound. Red soil would color the sea.

They walked cautiously in the river bed, expecting the enemy at every turn. By midday Penelope saw the sea. No boats were out, but below the last cliffs fishing boats must be waiting on their keels. Emmanuel and Katerina might be there. And the enemy, were they waiting? Were there motorcycles concealed in Mirtos, whose roofs would become visible at the next turning, or was the town, cut off as it was from the rest of Crete by the mountains, also cut off from the war? Alexis went ahead to the nearest hills above town. The others waited, but when the boy returned he could tell them nothing. The only thing out of the ordinary was a crowd going down the main street following a little girl draped in green branches. The crowd had followed her to the church.

Penelope said, "She must be a Perperouna. They're praying for water here, too." As a child she had longed to be the chosen one, the fairest child in town to carry the green branches to remind their Holy Mother that Crete was dry. But the weather had never been dry enough before, and now she was too old for such innocence.

To gain Captain Sefakas' house meant descending below the steep cliffs to the narrow beach. Even in daylight this was impossible except by way of the river bed, and for safety they waited until dark. Before the moon could rise they started out, slowly and quietly, the only noise coming from Old Markos, who puffed and complained, whose staff struck against stones and sent them rolling. The others kept hushing him. It did no good and in the end Penelope and Alexis converged on the old man. They practically carried him, against his protests. "Not this boy; I don't need his help." Alexis did not seem to hear Old Markos. At least he did not let go his grip until they had passed between the dark eroded walls which rose on either side and were on the sandy brink of the sea. Only then did they free Markos.

El Greco led them to a row of bathing shacks joined into one narrow house. A tang of salt, tar, seaweed and warm cork hung in the air. This was Sefakas' place and the shepherd tapped fearfully upon the door. There came a loud reply: "Yes?"

"That you, Captain?"

Again the great "Yes!"

They entered.

Captain Sefakas appeared undismayed by the invasion. He scrutinized them from under bushy brows—his eyes seemed almost in hiding—then sucked at a bottle through a yellow tube fashioned from an octopus tentacle.

"All right," he said, "what's up?"

"We are looking for people," said Penelope.

"That one's named Markos, right? You dispose of any sentries to get here?" asked Sefakas.

"Sentries?"

"Certainly, sentries posted on the cliff. Those Nazis are particularly thorough. They have sentries on the cliff to keep us from fishing and to make sure they've chopped holes in our boats. In a few moments they'll be here. It's routine, every night."

"Then you can't help us? You want us to go?" said Penelope.

"I think you had better go quickly," said the Captain. "Under that rug. There's a trapdoor; go there. Hurry, and be silent."

Beneath the trapdoor was darkness, a clammy cellar scooped in the sand. They fell into it and the trap closed on blackness.

Others were there, and among them were Emmanuel and Katerina. Penelope would have cried and laughed for joy but her father's hand closed over her mouth as a brisk knocking echoed from above. Booted feet strode the ceiling.

Thus the Metaxas clan became whole again. How

long it would last, none could predict. Only the past was certain. For several days Emmanuel and Katerina had been waiting here. They had taken the coast road after the trenches around Aghios Miron had been abandoned. The enemy, it seemed, was not interested in a small hill town. Now it was the future that mattered, an uncertain one at best. According to Emmanuel, the fishermen were willing to help. A few of the boats were being patched and on the first possible night they would escape. This was the plan, but there were difficulties and dangers. Many wanted to go and the boats were few. Before the escape occurred the partisans would be bringing down more refugees, wounded British soldiers who could not be easily hidden or cared for on Crete. Theirs was the first right.

There was the ever-present danger of discovery.

"They would never find us here," said Penelope.

"But they could very easily," said Emmanuel. He pointed out the possibility of an informer. Even rain might betray them. If it rained and the river flooded and overflowed its banks, the sand cellar in turn would flood. Then where could they go? Except for the river bed the beach was enclosed by the cliffs and the sea. Only a good swimmer would have a chance.

"Are there no paths at all?" asked Penelope.

"There is one," said Emmanuel, "a very narrow one that follows the river bed."

The path was known to very few and it was not safe. As long as the river was empty a solitary machine gun planted in the dry bed would command both river and path. No one could pass without being seen. Only if the river were pouring down the narrow gorge could the path be used and that was the last thing they wanted, to be flooded out of the cellar before the boats were ready.

Emmanuel said, "With this drought, I wouldn't worry about that." But El Greco said he believed it would rain and Old Markos agreed. His joints had a way of aching when rain was in the air.

Rain, discovery, or escape. They could only wait, through five days and nights of fear and hunger and boredom. Yet Alexis was oddly gay; he kept Penelope's spirits up. "Somehow I feel optimistic," he said. "I don't know why." And when the hours dragged he would try to amuse her. "Have you ever wondered whether cats eat bats?" he said.

"There aren't any bats down here," she said. Bats would be the last straw.

"Or whether bats eat cats?"

"What are you talking about?"

Alexis said, "It's from a book, *Alice in Wonderland*. Something to think about when you're bored. My mother used to read it out loud."

"You're fond of reading, aren't you?"

"I used to like her reading."

At other times tempers flared and arguments developed. Their greatest problem was Old Markos. He was rusting, he said. In Alexandria he would molder. When the partisans came with the wounded soldiers, he expected to return with them to the mountains.

Penelope knew her grandfather's intent was as sure of its direction as a train on a track. The only thing that could stop him would be derailment, death. It was not the habit of his mind and breeding to turn back. She saw him now as a menace, who through an excess of stubborn courage might destroy them all. Yet until these last days she had always thought of him as security personified, with a confidence that only children and dumb animals might share.

No one could dissuade Old Markos from his plan, and to make matters worse he badgered Alexis. Penelope could imagine the boy cringing in the darkness under the barrage. At these times she found herself counting "eight, nine . . . please make him shut up . . . twelve, thirteen . . . no more arguing, no more. . . ." But the wrangling went on and on, with Alexis moving from the defensive. He answered back, volley for volley.

"Listen, boy, when that bunch comes down you can have this spare gun. What a privilege to be with such courageous men and women. Their enemies will do well to fear them as long as they are above ground."

"Grandfather needs me along to carry him," said Alexis. "Otherwise he might go all squashy."

Markos said, "It might make you famous like me. You want to be famous later in life?"

"I never want to be heard of."

"Not a respected hero?"

"No, a coward."

They went on like actors in an unsuccessful play, doggedly giving what might be their last performance.

"Let me finish," said Markos. "So that you'll be known wherever you go?"

"I don't care about that."

"You're a cowardly whelp," said Markos. "A grandson of mine. . . . Well, why don't you curse me out? That's what I'm here for, to keep you simmering until you're hard-boiled."

"You're a noisy old man who won't live long, but I have my whole life ahead," said Alexis. "Old men can afford to be heroes." His voice showed no trace of anger, nor did his grandfather's. Strangely, although their disputes were frequent and the words bitter, it seemed to Penelope that they were better friends. As different as magnetic poles, they had begun to respect one another.

Worse than boredom and the long harangues were the hours of silent contemplation. Penelope's thoughts led her nowhere. They explored the same ground again and again, becoming so automatic that they dogged her sleep. If she could only find some reason for it all, this war. It seemed as though from the time of Cain and Abel men had gone on through the ages avenging wrong with wrong. There might be no more end to it than to the rise and fall of the tide.

This thinking was a new and painful process. If she could, would she have wished back the old simple life? Aghios Miron? Even if there were such magic in the world, she could not fit the old shell so easily. She had been away too long. To be with her family, that was enough to ask —Emmanuel, whom she adored uncritically, and Katerina. Penelope could put her arm round her mother now. In the dark, Katerina seemed a small, even vulnerable person. The Metaxas farm, that armor which had been Katerina's cold strength, was shorn away, leaving only the human being. For that beloved home they shared a grief which only women know. Alexis, too, had become part of the word *home* for Penelope, and El Greco, who had done so much while asking so little. With these beloved people nearby, she was at home.

The five days passed in this manner, and finally on the fifth their imprisonment ended as suddenly as it had begun. Without warning Captain Sefakas lifted the trapdoor.

"We're going," he told them. "I'm taking you to a sand bunker near the sea. Not a sound!"

fourteen

〒〒〒〒〒

They followed the Captain across the beach. Suddenly something exploded with a clatter of wingbeats from beneath Penelope's feet. Terrified, she made no outcry. The bird vanished in the darkness and she went on, heart pounding. On one side, the cliffs rose up pitch-black. On the crest lay Mirtos, a shimmering phantom in the first moonlight. A town clock struck repeatedly, but no one counted. They hugged the bank and waited while a crescent moon rose over the frosted sea like a toothless grin on an idiot's face.

"Now we can see better," whispered Penelope.

"So can they."

"I don't like the moon tonight."

"Everything stands so still."

"There isn't any wind."

"Not a sound."

Even Old Markos went silently. He was using Alexis as a crutch.

"If we could only hear them talking up there, or music on a gramophone," said Penelope.

"Even an owl."

"My Lord, but it's hot."

"It's going to blow up a gale," said the Captain to himself.

"So we'll fly all the way to Alexandria," said Penelope.

Four caïques lounged on the sand, their hulls patched with tar and canvas. Behind them tiny waves lapped the sand in little flurried gasps. The sea lay flat as a pane of glass beneath a silent barrage of shooting stars. All Crete was motionless, silent. No dog barked, no night bird sang. No light showed from the houses. Only the long deep swell moved the pebbles up and back, hissing under a gathering mist which suffocated the sea and pressed it flat. Penelope could smell the night odor of wild thyme, sweet and heady, rolling down from the mountains.

Captain Sefakas led them to a low dune behind which they could not be seen from the cliffs. Here they waited. No one spoke. Each had his silent hopes and fears. For Penelope there was her cherished island. Soon it would be gone, and yet she accepted this. It was not the end. She was going on. She had her loved ones and she had herself and somewhere their paths were fixed, though she could not know the way; it was too dark.

In the gloom strange shapes stirred. Were they only phantoms in that inner darkness that enclosed the terrors of the fugitives? Penelope strained to see, and saw nothing until something darker than the night loomed up in the blackness. Markos drew his guns, but Alexis snatched his arms, saying, "It's the woman!"

Crouched like a panther, Lady Messina came over the bunker and down among her recent guests. They shook hands silently. Torgut Bey followed her and Old Markos made a noisy fuss over him. "Here's something barbarous, something really savage!" he kept jabbering until Penelope hushed him.

From the dune's lip Penelope could faintly see black shadows stealing across the sand, carrying other shadows, helping shadows that limped or swung on shadow crutches. Those who could crowded around the caïques and sent them groaning for the water. The rumble of their hulls seemed loud as a cannonade and Penelope prayed to herself, "Please . . . don't let them be heard . . . please" until she felt a hand on her shoulder.

"You, Penelope—" It was Lady Messina. "Still worried about your friends at the convent? Well, don't any more. They're being looked after." There was no need for Penelope to speak; her appreciation shone from her face. "One other thing," said Lady Messina. "Do you still wish you were back there?"

"No, I'm where I belong."

Lady Messina stood up. She was addressing all of them now in a commanding whisper. "The lot of you, wait here. Everything seems to be working out. Keep your eyes on the cliff, and when it's time, we'll call." She scuttled toward the boats.

Alexis said, "With all those people coming down,

173

we've been lucky." But even as he spoke their threads of destiny were stretched taut and invisibly breaking in the darkness above them. It began with a thin growl of voices, a trample of feet, the clang of metal, then far away a bar of blinding light tore a hole in the night. Shouts rose: voices of insects and the chattering of a monstrous steel cricket.

"The machine gun!" said Penelope, disbelieving.

It fired from the river bed.

Searchlights swept the beach, etched boats and figures of partisans and soldiers as colorful cardboard cut-outs against the sand. The machine gun began knocking the cut-outs down while the partisans fired back hopelessly: Emmanuel with his shotgun, Markos with the pistols and the Turk with his antique rifle. They lacked range to reach the cliffs.

The old man prodded his grandson. The moon twinkled on the revolver as he offered it to Alexis. "Like it or not," was all the old man said, and with horror Penelope saw the weapon change hands.

Abruptly the firing ceased. There were no more targets, the enemy concealed behind the cliff, the partisans behind their bunkers. The partisans could not afford to wait, nor could they cross the sand because of the moon and the searchlights. No one dared stir except Old Markos.

"Sell your lives dear," he told them, and began to dig with the butt end of his gun, piling up the bunker.

Though Penelope had come to think of him as a danger, even a heroic caricature, the old man still had for her a splendor in this last fight. This was his element. She knew the same figure must have moved along the beach at Marathon and at Arkadion when Dervishes stormed the gate. In every dark hour throughout Greek history there had always been such a man, a lonely warrior moving through the fight.

For a moment his spirit stirred within her. It did not matter that they were trapped, that they had never fought on a beach. There was no choice. So long as they were there and held that ground, the beach was Cretan soil. Old Markos would die here if need be, and so would she. They might hold out all night and longer against the distant gunners, but the planes would come at last with their engines screaming. Then it would be over. There had been no planes when he had fought the Turks, but she knew he would fight them here, flat on his back with the gun propped on his knees to steady it, a new way of fighting for an old man who was not quite finished.

Abruptly the phantom war drum beat within her, then was silenced. There was Alexis, digging too. He hated war. What was he doing here? Had he fallen at last under the spell of Old Markos' fatal patriotism? Then her thoughts leaped ahead to the red-black bursting of the bombs, to death so incomprehensible and cold.

"It's like the old days, Grandson," said Markos. "We'll fight to the last."

"But we ought to be ready to fall back to the boats," said Alexis.

"To where? We'll fire into them as they try to get around us," said Markos.

Alexis asked, "What happens when they get behind?"

"We advance and win back the island!" roared Markos, not in poor jest but because it was what he expected to do. "You'll follow me."

"I'll be with you all the way," said Alexis. The gun was still in his hand.

The lull continued but Penelope, crouching behind the

sand, had no hope that it would last, or that it meant anything except that the enemy was preparing the assault. What were they doing here, waiting to defend a useless strip of sand she had never seen in daylight? They must not die here: somehow her world had to last another day, and another.

During this respite, two figures zigzagged across the beach with a twisting, turning run. Searchlights quickly followed them, and then the bullets. They dived for the bunker and the bullets spent themselves in the sand. The firing cut short, but the light settled over their shadow pocket, bright as day.

"Now listen," said Lady Messina. She sat down heavily, all her tiredness seeming to pass through her lips in a great indrawn sigh. "One of the boats won't float; the others are crowded with wounded men. There is only room for a few. Those who can fight will stay."

"It is not much of a choice," said Captain Sefakas. "It's taking a risk in those caïques with the storm coming."

To the east and south the sea was black, shielded from the moon by clouds which had piled up from the horizon and moved before the rain. Lightning pulsed deep inside.

"A dragon licking his chops," said the shepherd idly, as though he were lazing away the night with his flock on some deserted hill.

"If there is rain," said Alexis, "their light will be no help to them."

"No more talk," said Lady Messina. "Those who can't fight have to go as soon as the searchlights move away. Be ready."

Markos aimed at the light and fired, again and again. The light never flickered, but the machine gun cackled and sent a humming swarm overhead. He ducked down, cursing.

"All right, who's going?" said Lady Messina, the voice of doom.

"Katerina must go," said Emmanuel, "and Penny, and Alexis."

"Not my grandson," said the old man. "He stays."

"No, he's coming with us!" cried Penelope. "Alexis, remember how we talked about Alexandria and what we'll do there?"

Alexis held out his hand to her. Their cold fingers locked and squeezed hard. "Good luck," he said. The voice was taut with fear though the clasp had been resolute. "I'll see you one day."

"Oh, Alexis." If her hand had only been an iron band locked about his, but it wasn't and Alexis' hand pulled away.

"I think it was meant to end this way; maybe it's to prove something," he said, but there was no bitterness in his voice. He looked across the beach to where the boats were riding. The only flight left to him was with his eyes. They did not plead, merely looked, and Penelope knew that he was prepared to follow Old Markos, to do what was most against his nature. She did not know him. She had come to believe as he believed, and now he was no longer Alexis.

"Here," he said, "I have a present for you in this handkerchief. Go on, take it . . . say it's a present from a soldier. Open it later."

She took the package silently to hold it clenched in her fist as though it contained Alexis' life.

Katerina refused to budge. "It's better to stay and die here together on our island!" She threw her arms around

Emmanuel's neck and would not release him. "No, no, no!"

"You must, Katerina," he said, and forced her arms free.

"We've got to be ready," said Captain Sefakas, "the instant the light moves."

Two caïques had already pulled from sight. In a moment the last would leave without them.

"Now," said El Greco, his voice uncommonly sharp, "I'm going to move that light. When I shout, I want you out of this hole like a shot from a gun. That fast. Captain, please pick up that woman and carry her if you have to."

"What's this? What kind of magician's trick is the old fool pulling now?" demanded Markos.

"You're right," said the shepherd. "A foolish trick to make you laugh."

Penelope waited, not knowing what to expect.

Along the beach, firing had resumed. She noticed a few partisans had crept closer to the cliffs and were trying for the searchlights, without luck. One of the lights looked for them. The other fixed on the bunker.

Thunder rumbled and trickles of wind threw sand along the beach. Penelope thought she felt a drop of rain on her cheek, but it was only a bead of sweat.

"See you," said El Greco in a jaunty way, as though he meant soon. Before anyone could move, he was on the beach and running, shouting, waving his arms, across the sand toward the cliffs. The searchlight swung from the dune and glared down on the fleeing man while two figures scrambled for the last boat.

Penelope ran without a pack, without anything but what she wore. Holding up her skirt in one hand, she plunged through a nightmare world of sudden monstrous pictures, strange figures that rushed to and fro and stranger sleepers that sprawled in shapeless stupor deeper than sleep. Captain Sefakas followed, bowlegged under the struggling weight of Katerina.

The searchlights never saw them go. They beamed down on the shepherd moving diagonally toward the sheltering cliff. He was halfway there and the shells had not found him. He was still untouched when he came to the first jagged boulders jutting from the ground. Then sand jumped up all about his feet, a yellow cloud of it under the lights. He stopped and threw up his arms as a bird about to fly lifts its folded wings. The pulverized sand thrown up by the bullets enveloped the little figure and the lights swept back across the beach to where the last caïque was pulling out of range.

Penelope and Katerina huddled against the gunwale. They were safe, suddenly swallowed up in the rocking velvet tranquility of a Mediterranean night. Then Penelope unfolded the handkerchief which had all along been in her hand: Alexis' gift, six copper cartridges from an empty gun.

Beside them a Scottish giant with a dirty bandage about his head mumbled a Highlander's song. It should have been Alexis there. Penelope would have wept for her beloved cousin, who had no business fighting a war, but Katerina was already lost in tears and there was no one else to care for her. Penelope put her arm around her mother's shoulders. "They'll be all right, they'll be all right," she said over and over.

On the shimmering water where the boat had passed, spent shells threw a handful of silver coins into the moon path which Greeks call Christ's Way, where He trod when crossing the water to bless the fishermen. A phosphorescent trail spilled out behind like a comet's tail, and above, the wavering mast pointed out the last few stars.

A vast dark cloud had risen out of the sea. It towered higher and higher. The whole mass grew from within toward the summit as a loaf rises with the yeast. A prolonged splintering peal of thunder rolled across the water, shattering the stone surface of Crete and echoing back a hundred lesser voices. The rain came down with big battering drops, beating the waves flat. Water fell in torrents on the fishing boats, on the sea, on the island of Crete. It dampened the happy and upturned faces of the farmers of Mirtos, who dared the gunfire to go outside and rejoice, and it raised small puffs of dust in Aghios Miron before the mud came. It hissed on red coals in the bakery, waking the lame baker and his fat wife. They lay and listened to the sound. In Aghios Miron, the wells filled and the people were content, for the war had gone down other roads and passed the quiet town. In Heraklion it smoothed the edge of war, put puddles in the bomb craters, cleansed the scrap heaps where a captured convoy of trucks was rusting, ran down the barbed-wire stockades where prisoners shivered and put out tin cups to catch the wet. Farther east it beat down the mountainsides, which some say resemble the gray, armored back of a great sea dragon. Rain fell on the fields of a convent there, and the nuns knelt in the chapel. The rain flailed against the flocks of sheep, drove them together, sent them hurrying for shelter, but the wilder ones, led by the great horned rams, turned their backs to it and stood their ground. The falling night dimmed the strident searchlights, the shimmering spider legs which searched the beach below the southern cliffs and stung the faces of partisan fighters. There would be tales to tell of this night, of the grandfather as old as time itself and of the white-faced boy who led them there, against the storm-blind searchlights and the entrenched guns. The drops beat on the hard mountain soil and the shale and the stone could not hold the water, and it washed down into the streams. The streams flowed again into the rivers, which were suddenly full. All over Crete, the rivers rolled down to the sea with a roar like thunder.